WESTERN

T0094643

Originally published in French as *Western* by P.O.L. éditeur, 2005
Copyright © P.O.L. éditeur, 2005
Translation copyright © Betsy Wing, 2009
First English translation, 2009

Library of Congress Cataloging-in-Publication Data

Montalbetti, Christine.
 [Western. English]
 Western / Christine Montalbetti ; translated by Betsy Wing. -- 1st
English translation.
   p. cm.
 ISBN 978-1-56478-528-2 (pbk. : alk. paper)
 I. Wing, Betsy. II. Title.
 PQ2713.O576W4713 2009
 843'.92--dc22
                          2009016239

Partially funded by grants from the National Endowment for the Arts, a federal
agency; the Illinois Arts Council, a state agency; and by the University of Illinois at
Urbana-Champaign.

Cet ouvrage, publié dans le cadre du programme d'aide à la publication, bénéficie du
soutien du Ministère des Affaires Etrangères et du Service Culturel de l'Ambassade de
France représenté aux Etats-Unis.

This work, published as part of the program of aid for publication, received support
from the French Ministry of Foreign Affairs and the Cultural Services of the French
Embassy in the United States.

Ouvrage publié avec le concours du Ministère français chargé de la culture – Centre
national du livre.

This work has been published, in part, thanks to the French Ministry of Culture –
National Book Center.

www.dalkeyarchive.com

Cover: design and composition by Danielle Dutton, illustration by Nicholas Motte
Printed on permanent/durable acid-free paper and bound in the United States
of America

WESTERN

a novel by christine montalbetti

translated by betsy wing

Dalkey Archive Press
Champaign & London

CONTENTS

on the porch   3

at dirk and ted lange's place   33

the siesta   91

the duel   153

I
on the porch

1

Call him anything you want, this thirty-year-old in the checkered shirt who rocks back and forth under the roof of this porch in what can only be called a makeshift apparatus, haphazardly, with nothing like the harmonious movements of an actual rocking-chair—the slow movement of its curves in an ergonomic unity conducive to daydreaming—making do, under the circumstances, with this senescent chair, even being a little too hard on it, a chair covered in nicks and smudges telling of past carelessness (see that chipping, those splotches, the gashes on its rungs, the scars in its back), a rustic model (notice how thick the rungs are, the clumsy spindles fanning out), pushing it just a little bit too far, having wedged its back legs into a crack in the floor, while its front legs, like the lone two fangs, if you will, in some scarcely populated jaw, bite erratically at the ground, as though that jaw were snapping shut.

This haphazard snapping requires a driving principle working in alternation between balance and imbalance: our thirty-year-old's right leg is what provides this movement. Pushing down on the boot that rests on the horizontal rail built onto the front of the porch, well, it acts like a piston.

This precarious apparatus is kept in good working order by a modest but well-organized sequence of muscular activity, a whole series of motions, each muscle taking up where the last left off, at just the right moment (any distraction, any mistiming would result in a possible fall), and so, in this petrified dawn, deserted, seemingly frozen within a complete suspension of activity, utterly silent, there is only this imperfect rocking in the shade, only the scansion of the chair, to imply that all sorts of powerful forces are being called together, forces that—since the timing of the coming event isn't particularly important—we might as well keep on describing.

I'll summarize the situation for you. When the plantar muscles of our man's two feet start to flex as he rests on the rail, this engages, um, the triceps and the soleus muscles up in the calf. Our thirty-year-old, I'll go into more detail, relaxes the flexors of the feet, meaning, I think, the anterior leg muscle, and perhaps also, at the same time, the lateral peroneus longus, you can't exclude that possibility (I'm doing it myself, to try and feel what muscles I'm using, but even so, identifying them is not so easy). When you tense the knee, now, let's see how that works, it requires a semimembranosus as well as—there we go—semitendinosus relaxation, OK, done, and you can't omit the femoral biceps (as for the brachial, that's completely inactive, it just lolls around and doesn't participate at all). Stiffening the large buttocks muscle (come on now, no nervous giggles) then allows you to stretch your thigh while at the same time you relax the iliopsoas. Relax it. Good.

As for the rest, it's perfectly conceivable that there will be a slight abdominal contraction (I'll let you be the judge of that) completing the ensemble.

Only the boot, perhaps, the one resting on the rail, sticks out at all, because of the way it hangs off the porch, displaying its little leather mound, a hillock beginning to reflect the dawn, its delicate glow, still coming entirely from the horizon, still making its way up into the almighty ink, that's precisely the word, of the earlier nocturnal invasion. The boot's style is identifiable, with its beveled heel and the topstitching running up the leg in a wavy pattern—should we be seeing hills in all this stitching, their slopes full of game, their bucolic undulations so pleasing to the eye?—or is yours a more maritime imagination, leading you to think about the traces left by every obstinate returning wave on the sand of a beach—not the ribbons of foam that float on the air like fragments that have come loose from a mummy's wrappings (something you might come across on a very windy day), but those embellished drawings, those arabesques that that same regathering wave pours over: pulling back to consider what it's inscribed before coming again to scrawl some new figure with wild daubs of its brush, adding to its earlier lines in the sand.

In this lethargic morning, which will arrive in its own good time, and notwithstanding the boot and the rocking motion, which we've tried to explain the best we could, there really isn't all that much going on, and for the time being it's hard for me to tell you much more about it, unless we move closer to the rail where the boot is silhouetted and notice that, look, whereas we thought we'd already given an exhaustive count of everything falling into the category of movement, of life, in this scene, just look, there are quivering droves of hexapods here, scurrying around, traveling at their own pace, with the result being that we can, while we're waiting for this day to break, and for our man to stir—he still seems to be in some sort of vague interior space, from which the only thing we can extract is a mishmash of drowsy thoughts occasionally resolving into more precise snatches of monologue—we can always look down into their winding column, watching the mobile and regular dotted line it traces so precisely, and from a macroscopic viewpoint recognize that they're really something to see, with all those terebra, hooks, pincers, and other stinging parts, and look, check out that one there with its disgusting labrum that it raises and lowers in the morning air as if talking to itself, harping on some old idea it can't get out of its head.

Let's adopt their point of view for a moment (those not interested in animal life can skip immediately to Chapter 2 with no harm done).

Traversing the rail, if you want my opinion, can't be the most enjoyable part of their expedition, spreading their six feet over the chromatic monody of gray wood beneath them, its texture not particularly welcoming for anything not (as they are not) xylophagous. There is, however, if you think about it, something grandiose about their journey, because for a minuscule entity taking it into its head to cross the rail, wouldn't this stiff, woody support seem like the dried-up surface of a dead, arid planet, fissured here and spiny there, where splinters, yes, are as high as rocks, splendid peaks lifting magnificently to the sky? Aren't they actually a sort of astronaut, far from the earth, and wondering—those of them interested in science—about the possibility of life being able to exist on such bloodless terrain, where all you can see are looming empty craters and desolate mountains?

Yet, this existence of life, something most of them were skeptical about when they first set out, shaking their heads, alas, now looms there in front of them in the form of a vague, dark threat:

it's the boot, that enormous mountain of dark leather, radiating—they can feel it—some sort of heat, the heat of the human foot located inside, producing in all probability a diffuse caloric elevation that must circulate around the boot's outer limits like a halo.

Making their minds up right away—though if they were only concerned with advancing blindly, arriving more quickly, they could have scaled the aforementioned obstruction in order to take the most direct route—they skirt it by silent, tacit agreement, without first meeting in council to deliberate over the matter (imagine the disorderly jabber, the shrieks of objection, the vote, with the losers furious and a few of them perhaps beginning to wonder if it might be better to go it alone), the first in line taking it upon himself to make the detour, and each of the others following his lead without hesitation, with a docility that could make you wonder, was this the passivity, the scrupulous obedience of those resigned to having no opinions of their own, or, instead, seeing this great dark mass dangerously silhouetted in the middle of their path, were they all simply congratulating themselves on the decision of the first in line, on the wisdom he had been able to display once again and that had clearly saved them all from catastrophe—all they each had to do was take the detour, like their compatriots before them, rather satisfied with their guide and considering that a prudent later arrival at their destination was better than running the risk of massacre.

Because, yes, let's just imagine, if they had instead chosen to face the obstacle head on, having the gnawing feeling—whether due to ignorance or arrogance—that nothing bad could really happen to them on this nearly deserted dawn, or even, conversely, feeling inspired to have this sort of challenge thrust upon them by the foot inside its boot, motionless for the time being, and consequently deciding to brave the thing, what the hell, and beginning the ascent without too much difficulty, thanks to the adhesive qualities of their own feet, those same feet that could be counted in the hundreds, yes, just through their repeated tapping, delicate as it was—infinitesimally so, if you think about it—and which might have ended up provoking a tickly feeling on our thirty-year-old's instep, a feeling that would have given him no rest, put yourself in his place, until he stopped it, taking drastic and I fear irreversible measures, in this case lifting his boot up into the air to shake it and then knocking the rail with its heel several times in order to slay a portion of those responsible for this nuisance, leaving the survivors to escape any way they could, panic-stricken, heartbroken, disgusted at the precariousness of their existence, and, in mourning now for their many dead, waiting for our man to leave so they could come out and search for their shriveled little bodies.

And even if our hexapods' very light stamping wasn't something he could feel, can't we imagine our thirty-year-old—not feeling the literal tickling we've just now described—let's say metaphorically got pins and needles, his leg going slightly numb, tired of being up there for so long, so that, in order to wake up his sleeping circulation the leg engages in going up, whoosh, and back down onto the rail, this time with no dire purpose in mind, but lifting in spite of itself, when it goes up into the air, the column of those who at that very moment were crossing the toe and who, overcome with vertigo in the whirling rush, begin to slip, forming on either side of the shoe a helpless, swaying cord from which, sure enough, several links begin to fall, while those who manage to hang onto the leather no matter what are terrified to see the boot moving back down to the rail, and from their airborne viewpoint they can watch the different ways the others down below react, threatened with being squashed, some of them disoriented and fleeing in every direction, with no pre-established plan, others lifting their heads and opening bewildered labra, not really understanding, watching the heel's dark mass descend, their little morning monologues completely interrupted and not knowing how to react to the matter at hand, they who had followed the main part of the column unthinkingly, never considering the danger they were exposing themselves to, and who had taken advantage of their subjection, their mechanical obedience, to ruminate on a few personal thoughts in daydreams, plunging into these so deeply that now they can only panic; and the ones up above, hanging on, battling the nausea that the moving boot produces (so much swift, airborne motion must really take it out of you), as pale as if they were riding one of those terrible swings at the fair, anticipate the dreadful carnage to come, yet can do nothing and bid a mental farewell to those of their comrades who, scarcely perceiving what is about to happen to them, don't have time to get out of the way, alas, alas.

As for the one who seemed to be talking out loud to himself just now in the line, did he fare better than the others, or was he one of the missing—we can't know yet, in the confusion reigning on the rail, where some of the victims have been so deformed by the blow that you can no longer make out their features, others perhaps having taken advantage of cavities in the wood, crawling in and gathering up their little bodies the best they can, waiting in those tiny, unexpected caves for the shoe presently blocking the entrances to lift for good.

The ones who managed to escape have their backs to us, unrecognizable, a crowd already partially out of sight and indistinguishable from one another, unless maybe the one who looked like he was talking to himself is the one turning around, this time opening his lamellated labrum onto a soundless yawning gap, dumbstruck at the sight of this massacre and stretching his spindle-shaped and stunned antennae toward the dark mass of leather, wondering what could possibly have motivated such a bloodthirsty executioner.

Which mass of leather, in one final sally, raises itself again, making its dreadful shadow hover, a darkness wherein the ones still safe in their trenches hole back up, a few of them having stuck their heads out of their cavities as scouts before immediately diving back in (the dreadful spectacle of the rail surface sullied with those severed bodies), and this retreat was a good move, believe me, because the boot returns all at once to meet its shadow, to coincide with it, shutting in our survivors for the time being, with no provisions and only what little oxygen remains, while around the boot in the pale morning a succession of half-crushed bodies still writhe, begging as they desperately rally, in their final twists and squirms, for a few more moments of life.

Well, anyhow, at least we've escaped the worst, thanks to the prudent detour taken by our creatures, let's congratulate them as they slowly but surely make their way through what is in the end a perfectly peaceful dawn where each entity has its own place, the insects bustling around on the rail without encroaching at all on the chiropodic territory of our thirty-year-old who continues his frugal rocking, while the morning light, the true heroine of this crack-of-dawn, comes alive before our eyes, in a slow, sensual, overwhelming birth, a birth indeed, always inspiring for anyone up early enough to be its witness.

2

The second chapter opens with a description of the progress of the light making its heedless way through the resistant ether, making its leisurely way across the layers of atmosphere that are still for the most part filtering it out, given the angle of incidence, which, for the time being, continues to constitute a handicap.

But, though until now the color blue, with its low frequency, had been easily repressed in favor of a diffuse red, the latter is very visibly dwindling and, although the particles of oxygen, ozone, and water are still putting up their screen against the fragile, luminous flow struggling to break through, we are being plunged slowly into more subtle shades, while dawn drags on under porch roofs like long bruises that have begun to heal.

The knowledge that we, nonetheless, possess about the inevitable denouement of this conflict, waged by the valiant dawn against night, a conflict that, despite the initial disproportion of forces, will see dawn as victor in the end—unless the world is really falling apart—induces, of course, a rather passive attitude (it's not like you could help out and speed the process up), with the result that one lets oneself go a little, even me, waiting for the scene to become completely lit (a legend will be born from this shadowy magma), and you too, yes, you in allowing yourself be tossed about by these sentences, there you go, surfing on a main clause and then chasing after one that's relative, entering next into a temporal clause, smoothly, without troubling yourself, because you know that whatever you may perhaps have lost sight of will be returned to you when necessary, yes, you sled, you toboggan, you slide, leaving your worries behind, you have to, your grammatical concerns at least, all will become clear in due course, let yourself be carried along, there, there you go, you're riding on cushions of air, it's nice, it's cushy, I so much want you to be comfortable, to find these sentences as supple as any you could wish for, come on, give in to temptation, quit being so stiff, come on, there you go, easy now, easy, relax your body, I want you even more passive, more trusting, that's good, it should be as though you're on a little cloud, you're floating, you paddle around, come on, let yourself go, reading can be wonderfully regressive, yes, really nice, you let yourself regress, you bob along, you're a boat rocking all alone down these canals, you let yourself be pushed along, at cruising speed, you glance right then left toward the landscapes you're being offered, this is your time, a moment just for you that no one can come to take away, come on, give in, let yourself be carried, there, that's good, it's time for you to relax, I'm taking charge of things, not too abruptly I hope, I'm taking care of everything, trying not to be too heavy-handed, simply letting you, well, not drift, I'd be afraid that something bad might happen to you, that you might get lost, that you might stray too far from shore, so, not drift but float, float on your back on this slow current, which I'm making sure, that's my job, will take you where you have to go.

In this soft bluishness of a morning incompletely come to light, let's take stock. All things considered, as far as flora is concerned, there's nothing all that lively here, I'm afraid, only these livid thistles, drained of their chlorophyll, which are rolling around all dried up in the roadbed of the main street, bounding about incoherently like scrawny, wild rabbits. As for fauna, there's our anthropoid specimen still involved in the crude rocking described above. The rest of the inhabitants of Transition City are still holed up at this time of day behind the façades of their buildings, tossing and turning on bad beds, drooling on the collapsed bellies of their pillows (old withered stomachs that haven't eaten their fill for ages), their breaths whistling louder when they lie on their backs and then really roaring, leaving sound waves to swirl in the room with an astounding lack of affectation, a peerless abandon, a deafness to oneself that's really rather staggering, it would leave you speechless, believe me; they, in a word, fight firmly against the imminence of the day.

And I almost forgot the segmented and tiny bodies of our dependable hexapods, whose prudence we can only applaud once again because, well, let's take it a little farther, if we may, because, even though, just now, we put forward a hypothesis, realistic when all was said and done, in which the foot shaking itself up in the air—either because it felt the six-legged footsteps or because it felt the desire to get its circulation going—fell back onto the rail to massacre a large portion of our poor creatures, punished for having ventured into foreign territory, imagine what would have happened if the insects had begun, whether because they'd gotten lost or because they just wanted to take the scenic route, why not, or maybe even because they wanted to start a career in exploration, to walk the length of the boot's upper, and remember the topstitches undulating there, and how you could find traces of the sea in them, the imprint of where waves have licked a beach, so watch how those same waves, hidden and seething, might roll out again in a fantastic surge, reaching our insects and carrying off a few of the ones scurrying along closest to the edge, who, now, swallowing water and watching the land grow distant, giving up all hope of finding their brothers again, might end up letting themselves be carried along by the currents, for hours on end, for days and nights perhaps, closing their eyes on the spinning sky, the futile moons, the laboriously sparkling suns, until, let's hope, they reach a different shore where they might have had to begin their lives all over again, find food, negotiate a habitat, the ones already living there thinking to take advantage of this fact and indeed authorized by it to add to the immigrants' already considerable distress (I mean the grief of separation, the grief of the dreadful voyage, the grief of this involuntary exile forcing them to get used to all sorts of new parameters in life) the further insults of rejection, of denigration, of mockery, or just plain aggression, that's how insects are, but all of that, of course, is pure fantasy, the topstitching remaining just as it should, motionless on the boot, and our insects, as we have said, rather circumspect and unadventurous, having taken a detour that sheltered them from any such epic.

No, it's our man's thoughts, rather, that are at sea, having hoped to doze a little longer, telling themselves, well, they were going to be able to get up slightly after dawn, thinking that this was a very modest demand to make, they didn't really contemplate sleeping in because once the body was up they knew perfectly well that wouldn't be possible, but still, since the man had been able to get dressed by himself, automatically so to speak—because for a long time now he hadn't needed to have recourse to any cogitation in order to accomplish the movements that nonetheless, back at the beginning, remember, were such a headache and, well, there was even a period when people had to do it for you, sometimes providing a running commentary out loud during the whole business, and then, finally, when you'd begun to do it yourself, you weren't really very good at it, I'm afraid, you were shaky, inaccurate, getting your foot stuck in the cloth of a pant leg thanks to poor aim, managing only with difficulty the exact equilibrium required of balance and movement, yet doing a fairly good job of frowning, I bet you were reciting the various stages of the procedure to yourself so as to do it all in the right order, without leaving anything out; even now it can seem an awkward thing to do, sometimes, for example, you often lay tomorrow's clothes out on a chair, one by one, methodically, knowing you're going to have to deal with getting up pretty early, when thought will very likely refuse to cooperate, and there, on this day-before chair, you'll even (I'm revealing your little foibles) go so far as to arrange the clothes so that they'll be there for you in the exact order you'll need to put them on, the coat on the back of the chair, then the jacket on top, then the shirt, the pants on the straw chair's seat, and on the shirt the necessary underwear, and as for socks, I'm not exactly sure when they ought to come in, people have their own way of doing that, whether right after the underwear or once the pants are on, it's up to you—because, that is, the dressing process had apparently gone well, they, his thoughts, were pleading the case for a little extra daydreaming time, in no hurry to step forward to the front of the stage, perhaps leaning towards certain lascivious subjects—and, actually, it's a perfectly reasonable hypothesis, it's possible that, in this case, our thirty-year-old had kept most of his things on when he slept, which would have greatly simplified the mechanical work of getting up—since he had also, as far as I know, come down the stairs of the inn perfectly well, likewise without calling on his intellectual faculties, having, everything leads us to believe, a sort of body memory of the height of the steps; a memory that, you know, provides us with extra information about our man, indicating that he must already have been in residence there for some time.

So, consequently, we have avoided the scene that ends with our thirty-year-old slipping and finding himself flat on his back, *Mamma mia,* at the bottom of the staircase, waking up the other residents, and especially the innkeeper who would then have appeared with his candlestick, his white linen nightshirt, his mustache and, yes, let's indulge ourselves, a nightcap that droops down to his shoulder in the form of a mangy pompom he must tug at when he has insomnia since the aforementioned pompom looks like nothing so much as a small, scruffy, and unhealthy creature, half bald, and as far as the remaining fluff is concerned, just as disheveled as its owner, whose face with its bulging eyes our man would have seen suddenly looming above him, and then yours too, rather astonished at having walked in on all this, and you would have given a little cough, vaguely embarrassed by this mess at which you were forced to be present.

But no, behind this façade, something of the sweet heaviness of shared sleep prevails, and you can tell that everything's worked out fine, all by itself so to speak, and as for the chair, well, that senescent chair, not particularly favorable to delicate, fluid rocking, has in no way demanded that our thirty-year-old make use of his free will, he hardly went one by one through the available specimens standing idly in the inn's main room, testing their flexibility, evaluating the solidity of each seat with the palm of his hand planted firmly on the place you sit, no, his hand must have grabbed just any old chair and dragged it outside, simple as that, with no intervention by reason.

Consequently, his thoughts, who hadn't felt themselves necessary as yet, who knew that they shouldn't arrive too late to the party, did feel they had every right to hope for a slight prolongation of sleep, an extension of reasonable proportions, a little breather, that's all, if it wasn't asking too much, a bit longer under the quilt to let wakening come without a jolt, a time to swim between two seas, in a half-conscious state that would make the transition toward the daylight hours gentle for them, these same thoughts, and why shouldn't they, instead of finding themselves, as they now are, being subject to intermittent violence at the hands of the chair, dragging them violently from their dreams with its jerky rocking. The misuse of the chair produces a series of shocks, and that's what startles them, makes them begin to slide to the foreground, jostling one another, sometimes still protected by a corner of the quilt that they've been able to keep pulled up around them till now, providing a temporary defense, a padding, but for how long, and then oops, going backwards now, taking off in reverse, and with no time to pull the eider-down quilt onto their backs, they have a few nasty collisions, bouncing off the other side, and so on, so that, finally, it's a bunch of battered, bruised, clumsy, crippled thoughts, who never got the chance to emerge from their drowsiness, who now, black and blue, begin to come peeking through the curtain in a miserable procession.

You know the slow pace of morning thoughts, how, still heavy, they have a way of seeming to sink into the thick carpeted floor impeding their progress, or, actually, maybe it's more like soft caramel that sticks to their soles and holds them back, they have to fight through these enormous globs, have to struggle to pull themselves free of all that sugar, but, anyhow, getting them together is always a big effort, and then, in this instance, add to this normal, daily difficulty the incessant, repeated shocks resulting from the fits and starts of the not particularly comfortable, precarious rocking in which our thirty-year-old's body is engaged.

That's why, on this still-dawning morning (the blue expands—the particles with the most energy become more refracted as the angle of incidence changes), we're dealing with these poor battered thoughts, sore and sickly and hard to keep track of because it's hard to tell them apart—their expressions being rather pale, covered with nasty bruises—and they limp as they make their way forward, all bent over and unrecognizable.

Finally, all one can say about this—while the sapphire hue gradually becomes dominant—is that, among this troop of pitiful little thoughts, all bruised and indistinct, there's one that's steadier than the others, more robust, older, that fixes the gaze of our thirty-year-old on the wall in front of him, not because of any quality of the wall in itself, but because it is the ideal, neutral screen to project this thought upon; a thought unharmed by the jerky ups and downs of his rocking, a thought that was never made indolent by languid nighttime sleep, but remained strong and sure of what it wants, a thought whose power is at least partly based upon its longstanding and proven perseverance. We ourselves still know nothing about this key and almost authoritarian thought, but, let's face it, it's not hard to figure out that said thought is what will provide the overall motivation for our man, explaining his days in this place and lending his mind a purpose that, unknown though it is, no doubt forms the horizon of his life wherever he may be, and which—we can tell from the sort of tension persisting even in his early morning apathy—he must never let out of his sight.

You can see pretty well now, you can even see perfectly, the sky is completely blue, punctuated by the white fluff of small, neat cirrocumulus, a really nice effect, and so I think the action can begin.

3

And while the procession of cirrocumulus visible above the scene presents the same docile and organized image as the perfect dotted line of our hexapods, all advancing in the same direction and keeping regular spaces between themselves, between one cloud and the chubby, cottony mass of the next, whose texture could, at this early hour, make you think they were actually the wooly stuffing from your own pillow, somehow escaped, our thirty-year-old, suddenly coming to life, musters with a start all the forces of vigilance that make one more or less present in a given situation.

Regaining all at once the small stock of those ordinary faculties that usually serve to respond more or less correctly to the various stimuli the outside world transmits to you and that, speaking generally, allow you to engage in even the simplest and most modest activities that arrive one after another to fill out the content of the day, our thirty-year-old undertakes an optical review of the wall where his one independent idea had become stuck like a lump in the paint and concealed that vertical plane above which the frieze of our sky speckled with its impeccable ornamentation is so nicely in motion. With that upper frieze thus safely suspended, his gaze descends to the one supported by the horizontal ribbon of the main road, where it disentangles itself, look, from the tumbleweeds that the wind rolls along the sandy surface, in order to follow the progress of a completely different entity, a piece of brown paper, the sort used to wrap what the locals would call *doughnuts*, and that's living (this is hypothetical) through a sort of identity crisis, during which, without access to its own image, it thinks it's a tumbleweed like all the others, and is doing its best to hop along in their midst. Almost the identical color and practically the same mass, it gets right in the middle of a troop of dry thistles and, thinking that it's found its brothers at last, leaps happily along as morning begins.

Our thirty-year-old, distracted by this sight for a moment, a sight that nonetheless allows him to sharpen his still burgeoning faculties, you know what mornings are like, is trying, inwardly, to put the finishing touches on a plan to execute an extremely simple project, a project that will likely come to fruition long before that other, old, fixed, principal idea of his is given its satisfaction (judging by its hearty constitution, by how old it looks, this idea probably requires that a whole series of other conditions be established before it can be successfully enacted, conditions we can't really guess at this early in the day, but which, clearly, have not yet come about); this particular project being that much easier because, having already completed it successfully a certain number of times, our thirty-year-old knows he's up to it; a project that, for a whole damn litany of mornings now, he's planned out carefully and hardly ever failed to accomplish; a project that—we might as well just come out and say it—consists of paying a visit to Dirk and Ted Lange.

He lets the project hang there a bit, a pleasant notion, like an aroma you breathe in with a joyful hunger, knowing it won't be long before you taste the dish producing it, like the nebulous wisp rising from a cup—right?—that you contemplate with a satisfaction that derives not so much from steam's slender, filmy way of undulating harmoniously in the air as from the anticipation you feel for the sweet, fragrant warmth that will arrive like the lick of a warm breeze on your face when you drink from it; and right then and there, here we go, employing an abdominal contraction with an effectiveness that needs no further description, lifting his right leg, whose foot leaves the railing to set itself down on the floor, flexing in succession—one, two—the plantar arches, and with the usual swing of his arms, he leaves the porch behind.

The motion of his ambulation then adopts the alternate deployment of his two lower limbs in a manner that doesn't really call for commentary, except perhaps in the slightly bowed curve to his legs, or maybe the familiar, rather awkward gluteal friction impeding said ambulation a bit (a seasoned eye would probably see this as evidence that these two lower limbs are not the thirty-year-old's most frequent mode of locomotion).

He doesn't walk in the direction of the windmill, towards which—who knows—you might have preferred that he go, appreciating the way its poetic silhouette stands out against the naked landscape, without your necessarily being able to explain its attraction, which derives as much from the mobility of its blades (whose circular movement, this is your considered opinion, embodies a brief discourse on time—passing, turning, perhaps coming round again—a discourse you would have a hard time interpreting, all things considered, but that takes hold of your feelings in a way that is not entirely disagreeable to you) as from its great stature, making its presence there more forceful, almost protective, but, rather, in the opposite direction, toward the other end of the main road, beyond which lies the ranch, a little way back from the road and at a slight angle in relation to the buildings that line it.

This morning walk, necessitated by the material continuity of spaces—something you can't just dismiss with a snap of your fingers in the real world—will also give you a chance to meet some of the residents who have now properly woken up and whom you can sometimes see or even greet as you pass their doorsteps, or else, if still inside their homes, see attending to various things, their curtains not drawn but rather letting the natural light come through their windows in short, welcome waves of photons that splash into their dark rooms.

Introducing Thomas Burnett, his physique carved like a whittled wood whistle: roughly, that is, without attention to detail, with a few mistakes here or there, a few slips of the blade that, as it scraped away, introduced slight asymmetries that are immediately noticeable on first encounter, but then—the result of a remarkable structural economy—fade more and more as they become familiar, until they almost disappear, accentuating the intelligence of his expressions, so that you naturally begin to delve deeper and deeper for their likely meanings, when you converse with him.

So, good morning Thomas Burnett, who returns this hello with a quick, preoccupied wave of his hand, because behind you his eye has caught sight of that piece of brown paper hopping along in unison with the tumbleweeds, coming into its own in the midst of their flock, now growing bolder, heading down the road alone in little absentminded leaps that call it once again to the attention of your gaze.

But this vision is too ephemeral to allow for positive identification, your silhouette blocks the situation somewhat, so Thomas Burnett's mind returns to his morning's itinerary without giving this chimera another thought.

Next we have Jeff W. Dunson, whose eyes, probably too close together to take an interest in anything aside from each other, don't even try to meet your gaze, to put it mildly, in fact turning his entire face away from you in a strange sort of twist more appropriate to a fish swimming past a diver, for example, and naturally having no particular interest in looking him in the face, why would it, thinking, really, it's much better to pass on by, to the side, as casually as possible, making sure there's a way out if, perchance, the aforesaid frog-man happens paddling around down here with some intention less aesthetic (admiring the supple curve of its flexible though scaly silhouette as they pass one another) than bellicose, aiming a harpoon or knife at the creature, so that the fish is quite delighted now with how its swerve has left the field open for it to turn, splash, away to the left, so that the diver's right arm, blocked by his body, can't manage to get at it in time.

Next Nordman, Will Nordman, greets our man—who's directly in his line of sight to the windmill—with a laconic wave and, after the parenthesis of this brief distraction, plunges his gaze once again into the large spherical face of the impeccably paced wheel capping off the potbellied basin below and positioned on four feet, planting it firmly, a sentinel, ready to get down to work, Nordman thinks, and its placid, distant silhouette continues to suck away the better part of his attention.

When you walk by the General Store, isn't that Harry's acromegalic silhouette busying itself behind the windowpane, digging around in his merchandise to check the stock, a body you only see in fragments now, chunks, figures that turn, revolve, changing their surfaces and contours in such a way as to render them difficult to grasp, hard to interpret.

So you continue past Harry as well, his metamorphic geometries swept by bright flashes of light that also seem to be in motion, moving from point to point on the surface of the curtains at the whim of the moving folds that slash or flute the cloth.

It's an entirely different matter when you reach the next window and cast a casual eye toward the dark interior, where, thinking you won't see in there any better, your eyes encounter the gaze, close and sharp—driving immediately and directly into your own—of Jim Hopkinson, whose taut, stationary posture makes you guess that he takes up this post every morning, because he's come to enjoy catching eyes by surprise as they dawdle into his space and then fastening them to his, handcuffing them, clack clack, so that here you are—tetanized, transfixed by a sort of fleeting guilt, riveted to Jim Hopkinson with a dependency that you can't explain, as if you owed him some debt for having thought that you could with impunity fill your retinas with his personal or physical property, and you let the eyelids at fault drop down over your eyes, now lacerated by the sharp edge of his gaze, and they cover them loosely, offering their modest protection, the slender rosy curtain that you draw modestly against the world.

And when your eyes reopened reach the surface of the road, the handcuffs break and set you free.

The penultimate sight, Burt Livingstone's deeply creviced face and two matching ears, which have such immense, flat, fleshy lobes by comparison with the average (and without taking my own into account, they're unusually narrow, I have to admit, and therefore unacceptable as an accurate measure of normality) that they seem to form two miniature canyon landscapes on either side of his face, where you could, if you wanted, follow the shattered outlines of innumerable little fissures (ah, those wrinkled faces that seem to have been put here simply for us to read, which you could sit happily and let your mind wander in for hours, believing you can decipher in the lines of every wrinkle the extraordinary, secret account of a life . . .).

But you don't have time for that, you have to follow close on the heels of our thirty-year-old, quick, don't lose sight of him, because what would we do, I ask you, stranded in Transition City, if we had to track down our own hero, who would have shaken us off, quite unintentionally, thanks to our own distraction and tendency to linger as we walk.

Quick, because if we just hang around open-mouthed in the face of all these new sights, how will we know where to go, since we don't dare—in our rough approximation of English—ask the way to the ranch (would that even be prudent in these parts, where it's always best to seem to know where you're going?), nor to show up there alone without the tacit recommendation of our thirty-year-old's company . . . quick, unless we want to stay here wandering aimlessly on the sandy road while waiting for our thirty-year-old to reappear somehow or other, in a few hours maybe, come on, hurry up, please, let's content ourselves with these small sketches, and now the urban landscape is ending and here comes the final energumen to offer us his opaque silhouette, John Burns, who greets you without paying much attention, bending over to pick up a piece of brown paper littering his doorstep and considering it dubiously in the palm of his hand—our piece of brown paper, its surface all sandy, pricked and scratched by wild thistles, exhausted from running and now landed here, completely out of energy, lifted by this arm-crane to where John Burns can see it, then crumpled, crushed, and broken in the hand now leading John Burns's whole body back inside his house, where he's about to throw it away.

Our thirty-year-old, his long shadow crinkling on the uneven ground, duplicating him in an elongated double, crosses the town line, dragging this imperfect twin at his heels, its turbulent contours hugging whatever random, irregular volumes it happens to be projected upon, its fluid outline spawning temporary excrescences, edemas, buboes, serrations, fringes, and other flourishes.

And because of the quarter turn he makes to the right, this shadow, approximate but docile, changes now in perfect synchrony into a profile silhouette whose gray pool opens out onto the single step marking the entrance to the ranch.

II

at dirk and ted lange's place

1

So now here you are in the small courtyard where you sit opposite your old friends Dirk and Ted Lange on a lame chair with its
feet scraping a ground composed of white gravel chips, rapidly
losing out to and vastly outnumbered by the white sand that is
their nemesis in this district.

I say your old friends, but I should have said your old friend
Dirk and his brother Ted, whom you find agreeable company,
you like his relaxed attitude, his way of being there in that small
courtyard each time as though this particular place was obviously the only proper place for him, as though there could be no
better spot than this little courtyard, this corral, and yet Ted, the
least sedentary of these two cowboys, has eyes that are haunted
by a recent memory: and here we can insert a reverse shot of the
Lange herd's summer pastures, where the cattle munch in abandon, nothing to restrain their herbivorous instincts now, crunch
crunch, while the silhouetted mountains provide an impeccable
scalloped background for the scenery, the upland pastures where
Ted drives their herd with exactly the same ideal choreographic
emphasis, the same ease of motion, the same perfectly balanced
coincidence between his body and the space it occupies—*lucky
him!*, I think the locals would say . . .

But it's the other one, Dirk, the close-mouthed one, his face
always creased, always tired in advance, for whom you feel
friendship, he being the one, with his way of seeming to be
tangled in his chair rather than sitting, knotted like spaghetti
that got stuck together when it was cooked, and with a tempera-

35

ment we'll call reserved, that, who knows why, has won your friendship, this man who now, look at him, is making no verbal progress whatsoever, his words tied in terrible knots, oops, stumbling, tripping on all sorts of imaginary stumbling blocks that collide with his voice, a disaster, falling all over themselves, faltering, the same man who, after a few inconclusive attempts will—as usual—give up on participating in the exchange that will, in his absence—or rather, in his almost petrified presence—move very quickly, so that, instead of contributing energy to their conversation, he adds weight to it, ballast rather than stimulation.

Each time your gaze moves across Ted's face, though what am I saying "his face" for, I mean his whole person, the way it sits on its chair, each time that you contemplate what it's expressing via its posture, contemplate the likely meaning of the kind of ideogram that his body is delineating, one arm with its elbow casually on the back of his chair, a supple outcrop (nothing in common with Dirk's when he attempts the same position: narrow, pointed, hooked, looking no better than a chicken wing), legs crossed to take up the maximum of space (see how the one with its ankle on the other knee creates a wide triangle), his limbs occupying (this is the obvious conclusion that comes to mind) the greatest possible volume given the narrowness of his support—with the result that the meaning of this ideogram is not at all opaque but perfectly readable, opening out into a brief and easily translated statement concerning a particular manner of filling up time and space, a relaxed and happy manner, inscribed precisely into the surrounding décor: finding his place as though everything had been made for him, as if made-to-measure, but without arrogance, quite the opposite, offering you a tranquil, welcoming example that opens out, in fact, into a sort of pedagogy of space and time, one you would do well to imitate, not overwhelming you but just inviting you to do the same as he, drawing you into itself—each time you undertake to catalogue this man systematically, who fits into this place so successfully, you register all the objective reasons for possible friendship; and despite this list (which inwardly you find quite persuasive) and the compound causes for its various entries (which we won't bother enumerating)—far more numerous, really than the reasons you might be attached to Dirk—whether because of the chance order of encounters, whether it's a matter of chronology, history, and the density that time provides for relationships, with the result that the sum of the moments passed in one another's company forms, as one moment leads to the next, the foundations upon which a friendship may begin to rest confidently (so that when you see this friend, let's admit it, you're also seeing the bits and pieces of these past days, reassembled—because time also has the function of binding you, doesn't it, to people, and whatever you might say on the subject, you always let yourself be ensnared with a certain delight by the familiar)—or whether the reason is something so ethereal and evanescent that it's able, here, to make a convoluted escape . . . anyhow, I know I'm quite right in saying that it's Dirk, really, first and foremost, who has to be described as a friend.

That Dirk and Ted are twins in no way increases our confusion, especially since it just so happens that these two individuals, endowed with a feature-for-feature resemblance at the beginning of their lives, apparently drew lots one day, in a childhood pact, for all the available moral characteristics, all the ways of behaving that they could imagine, to split them up, one for you one for me, divvying them out once and for all and leaving nothing unclaimed.

Their characters, then, being so opposed, led them to animate their faces and their bodies—despite these being exact duplicates—with the equivalent tendencies, so that they appeared radically different, a posteriori: a difference that, through such singular use of their personalities, had by now become physical in nature.

Their smiles, just as an example (a census of all the differences engraved now in the sign language of their faces or the contours of their bodies would take a long time to write up), spread their mouths into very different curves, Ted employing a vigorous, straightforward muscular contraction, stretching without hesitation the ribbons of the major and minor zygomatics that roll the corners of his lips up like straps on well-oiled pulleys, while Dirk only ever offers you a meager, crooked smile, minimal, even metonymical, an allusion to the act of smiling, with which one must learn to make do.

Anyway, a probably superfluous detail, but let me say, one shouldn't take the description "an old friend" as providing any real information as to time or age—neither with regard to the twins themselves, who are no doubt close to being thirty-year-olds themselves, nor with regard to the chronological substance of the friendship, which only goes back a few seasons, at an estimate—no, it's an affective term, used the way you would expect, a somewhat old-fashioned way of speaking and pretty much part of the atmosphere of this fable.

Let's take a moment to look at the little courtyard a bit.

Imagine something crude, geometric, something marked out by broad, simple lines, the results of the primary volumes of the space involved.

Only two of its sides (let's say A and B) are fleshed out, their substance being, for A, a low wall approximately five feet tall (a seated man—and here we have three of them—wouldn't be able to see over it), for B, the façade of the house, joined on the perpendicular by this low wall. The other two sides (thus, C and D), immaterial, have to be deduced, mentally, following the property's orthogonal signals, without these invisible limits ever quite lining up with the vague frontier of jumbled gravel chips, some part of which have been able to roll outside their perimeter, as if, to even things out, they're trying to make themselves just as abstract as those entirely conceptual geometric boundaries.

As for outdoor furniture, a table, four simple chairs, that's all that's been asked of you, with the white light of noon gathering the human shadows directly beneath the people here, where they hide as though the heat were too much and they had to take shelter, huddled, under the bodies they belong to. Shy, shrunken, condensed, prudent shadows, without the least bit of swagger, and with none of the ostentatious extravagance of their late-afternoon colleagues, nor the languid appearance of the morning ones.

Three bodies, somehow persisting in an environment that's truly as bare as they come; an environment that it would be a good idea to imagine more closely, without, however, adding anything of your own—a flimsy Chinese paper lantern would hardly be acceptable, for instance. Carefully, carefully now, don't lose control and fill the place up with crazy imaginary decorations. At the very most you have a free hand with the bumpy spots punctuating the rough surface of that short wall, you can distribute snags and grainy patches wherever you like, to signify either the inevitable erosion of things (that's just like you) or else perhaps isolated mechanical events, the scoria accumulated by time; you can turn a mason's eye on it, if that appeals to you, and if some slight zoological impulse leads to some lizards crawling across it, go ahead, they won't bother me, they'll make a quick getaway just as soon as they meet our gaze.

Within the space of this courtyard, which we've now defined fifty percent by material means and the remainder by mental ones, a few remarks have begun to be exchanged, functioning, how shall I put it, less to circulate any noteworthy information than to create a basic verbal foundation upon which to establish the silence that will follow, a silence into which—thus authorized, and needing no more proof of conviviality—they can all plunge freely each going on now with their own private, unimportant thoughts.

Busy with providing the basis for this silence to come, Dirk, whom I am happy to introduce (tall, scrawny beanpole, you say to yourself when you first swap glances with him, unable to prevent yourself from summing up what you see in a single characteristic, in order to get a fix on things), Ted (with your trained eye and in a lightening quick inventory, you gauge his similarities and differences with the former at the same time as you gladly shake his hand, Hello Ted), and our thirty-year-old—who, thankfully, has indeed arrived ahead of us—(Ah yes, we've met, you say, interrupting the handshaking gesture that you'd absentmindedly half-made as they were introducing you, there, you retract your right manual appendage, hup!, and stick it in your pocket to disguise your lack of composure, while with a panoramic glance you reappraise the situation, Dirk, Ted, our thirty-year-old, everything's perfectly under control now), launch into a few direct remarks to one another, each according to his own abilities.

Because previous conversational experience doesn't always go without saying, our three men, confronted with this difficulty, find that they aren't equally matched.

Especially the two brothers, the division of functions and qualities that they apparently long ago achieved leaving one taciturn and the other voluble, though the taciturn isn't taciturn on purpose, it's clear that he works hard to maintain his position like anyone else in the conversational exchange, that like his neighbors (a bit less often, perhaps, with less conviction, less confidence, less spirit, it's true) he tries to catch, in a manner of speaking, the ball, whenever it seems to be aimed toward the zone he's responsible for, but usually it goes high, wow, way too high (you can see him make a slight, futile jump for it, his hands stupidly held out in front of him, his arms open wide as if to hug it). Or else he barely misses it, it skims past his outstretched fingers, it simply burns their tips, which are reddened in the attempt; and even when there's a better spin to it, and his fingers manage to send the ball back—I'm taking advantage of the fabulous possibilities for metaphor, here—they do so without enough energy, so that the leather projectile lands with its inflated air bladder outside the net on his own team's side, where an awful grumbling arises, a cacophony buzzing in his ears, in which he manages nonetheless to distinguish one or two decisive, heart-searing tirades. Or else he reaches his two arms out in a triangle closed by his joined hands, ready to make an offering, running to meet the projectile which comes as expected to strike the sacrificial plate of his connected thumbs; but, instead of flying up in a magnificent rebound, the ball only seems to make a brief stop in its fall, and there's our Dirk with his thumbs hideously bruised, the veins beginning to stand out, delineating their pale green and swollen net on the surface of his skin, and the ball, for all that, still being difficult, rolls onto the ground—and memories come back to you of summers, of fields, of grass, of nets stretched between two trees, of situations when it hadn't been possible to get out of the game (now you're thinking, one thing leading to another, about real games), either because they insisted, Come on, let's go, demanding your participation, urging you on, It's not going to hurt you, or because it seemed too difficult to you, in this particular instance, to admit that—personally—you weren't really too interested in injuring your hands batting around a too-heavy ball or twisting your neck as a result of watching airborne trajectories just in order to predict where the thing would come down, really, it didn't interest you at all; but in the exhausting sweetness of summer evenings you had to do your body the slight violence of moving quickly in response to the random fits and starts demanded by the game and to endure the shock of the leather ball against your fragile hands, a violence also done to your dreamy interior monologue that could no longer continue to be comfortably unfurled, though it's not impossible that, here or there, it still found a way of popping back up, raising its mischievous little head while the ball was with the other team, or more luxuriously, taking advantage of the fact that the ball had rolled on the ground and one of the players had gone to get it, not running, pounding the earth as though each step were a lash of a whip he was wielding in expiation for not having returned quickly enough with the airborne but heavy object that with the force of its speed and weight separated his hands and fell between them as if they were a basket with a hole in it; a monologue (I'm talking about yours) that usually has to be focused on the ball, which darts left and right instead of rippling along at its own rhythm; while, for example collapsed in a white polyvinyl chloride chair with cushions—striped in royal blue and mallard green for only a little extra—or, another of your favorite positions, sitting at the foot of a tree (this propensity for laziness used to drive your parents crazy when they noticed it), you could have peacefully considered the spectacle, always somewhat strange, disconcerting, agreeable, vaguely pictorial—for someone who's come from the city—of nature.

2

So Dirk, the one we've called the "old friend," feeling pretty small right now, bravely endeavors to participate in the conversation, looking all around for words as though they already existed somewhere in a solid state and just had to be extracted from whatever out-of-the-way place they're hiding in.

Without beating around the bush, he sets off in search of terms that, despite his vigilance, continue to loiter in the margins with no intention of making an appearance, and when he happens to find one of them, he grabs hold of it for you by the scruff of its neck and drags it, without further ado—struggling because of the weight of this cumbersome, limp individual, resisting him with all the power of its passivity—all the way up to the mouth that opens to submit the prisoner to Ted and our thirty-year-old.

Thus reaching the harsh light of the courtyard, the not-very-cooperative word blinks its eyes and takes shelter behind its arm against the surge of photons rushing onto it, hesitating briefly, right there, while a second one, we have to hope, emerges behind it in turn, propelled the same way, its face equally chalk-white, with that same grimace our faces always take on when shrinking away from such luminous aggression—as if the idea was always to present as little surface area as possible to the enemy.

A few more are caught in the dragnet like this and end up riveted together by a bunch of conjunctions that link them like chains, like ankle irons, until finally a whole troop of puny convicts stands there in the overexposed space of the ranch.

And our thirty-year-old, how is he making out in this exchange? well, he's preparing to make his own entrance into the conversational game—see that word pawing the ground impatiently inside him?—still holding back, but full of a promising energy that stands out against the background landscape of his thought.

This word of his, having left a group of other words behind it, collapsed in a heap—the ones preferring to hang around in parietal darkness rather than see the light of day—is making its lonely way through his mind. It's tried in vain to convince its fellows to follow, exhorting them, telling them—still huddling in their damp caves—about the beauties of the outside world. Over there, it told them, the air is clear, the horizons limitless; over there you go at your own pace, you skip along and people watch your every move, they contemplate and consider you; sometimes you'll even be greeted with an admiring whistle—you'll surf with unimaginable joy on the crest of this exhalation—and then other times they'll weigh you gravely, making small motions of approval with their heads, and in the hollows of their hands you'll bounce back as supply as though you'd been launched from a giant, deep, and springy mattress; a warm look will emerge from between the two limits of their eyelids and envelope you as you fall back into their hands like a beam of light in a clearing; over there, yes, out there, it said, trying once again, but the other words grumbled and went back fuming to their cave where they lifted a limp hand to signify Enough, enough! before fluttering lazily through the stale air back onto their straw mats.

Well if that's the way you want to be, you worms, just keep on crawling—it had decided on saddling up its horse, a little annoyed because it couldn't enlist its compatriots, a little annoyed because it had already been picturing itself at the head of their expedition, bravely leading them forward, meeting each danger with a strategic response, guiding them to safety in the end, at which point they would naturally have felt a strong sense of gratitude, even the ones that might sometimes have balked at blindly obeying their leader's orders, that might sometimes have tried to question its tactics, one or the other asking its traveling companions suspiciously what the reason could be for this or that obscure operation, the ones that had worked up the courage to voice some boldly pompous advice on the subject, later realizing their own plans would have been disastrous, and all of them extremely happy in the end to be back with their leader, because their leader had such clear-sighted opinions about everything, and consequently, from then on, they would be ready to move heaven and earth for it if ever this was needed.

So, alone, at its own pace, moving into those dark lands where its horse's shoes were constantly in danger of slipping on the mossy rocks, confronted by the thousand traps laid by the protophytic microorganisms that were slyly taking pleasure (it thought) in creating the slipperiest possible texture, spreading themselves out in treacherous patches that would appear where they were least expected, it had climbed pensively back up to the opening of the thirty-year-old's mouth, where at this moment it is finally preparing to cross the boundary.

For a moment it stops at this obstacle; not that it's hesitating, but it has to figure out the right amount of force to put into action—heels in its mount's flanks—to break through. It takes advantage of this pause to set in memory the scope of the heroic action it's just about to accomplish, so that it will be able to think about it later, revising it when there's nothing much to do, having like everybody else its own rocking chair to sit in at twilight and consider the course its life has taken. It runs a panoramic glance over the oral cavity—the granular walls, the dark pink surface—from the mat of the tongue, where its mount's foot is sinking slightly in. And then, there it goes—it crosses the enclosure of the teeth, takes the labial gate in stride, and then lands in the midst of the three friends, a Lilliputian rider fallen into a gigantic setting, emphasized by the considerable silhouettes of our three Gullivers, who then thoughtfully consider it.

Dirk spoke up in reply. His mind, working a little better now than it had a moment before (but also showing signs of the high level of difficulty, subjectively speaking, it found in the task at hand), now a little better equipped, cast long metal chains ending in harpoons into the grottos where reluctant words seek shelter. Not to be outdone, crampons and grapnels soon complete this ferocious arsenal.

Dirk brandishes these threatening and prehensile curvatures, sending them down toward the shadowy depths where language sleeps. Several words, sleeping there and not expecting the efficient use of any such apparatus—thanking their lucky stars and telling themselves that they would always have plenty of time to hide farther away if they should ever hear the mind's first vengeful steps as it set out in search of them—are very quickly speared.

This swift operation, the nice quick job of fishing them out, brings these words immediately to the surface, where it seems, well, what else could you expect, that some of them have been damaged in transit. They emerge with some visible deformities, bearing an *O* in their midsections where there should be an *A*, suffering from a missing consonant at their extremities, even with an entire syllable amputated; and that's how they enter the conversation, bruised, incomplete, mournful.

By means of all sorts of gymnastics, they hoist themselves to the tympani of the two listeners and make their way forward by crawling on their elbows into their auditory canals, then up to the area of the brains seeking to interpret them, where they are examined quite dubiously, turned over every which a way in systematic attempts to decipher them, until finally one of the additions or substitutions contemplated in the course of this experimentation leads to a word listed in the dictionary. This word then reemerges with its new prosthesis, decked out in this addition or substitution, either from Ted's mouth or that of our thirty-year-old, and followed by a questioning pause that makes its mark visible—a stunted crosier—in the air: *Is it . . . that you mean*? And then the rehabilitated, the complete word, enters into Dirk's auditory canal in turn, with—we have to admit—a certain nimbleness, alert, hale, and hearty, where it is instantly identified as correct and filed away, while a *Yes, yes* finds itself sent back out in its place; or else, if judged improper, it is rejected as such, dragging in its wake a *No, no* that finally shoves it aside, and the initial, mangled word then finds itself sucked back into the ear of one or the other of our two listeners, who revise it again and end up extracting a new formulation from it in the same bucco-laryngeal manner, and now endowed with its brand-new transplant, this proposition is considered in turn and so forth, until the *Yes, yes* of happier days is reestablished. Or perhaps even Dirk himself, willing to provide a little post-sales service and support, takes the incorrect word back, unscrews the faulty addition, reconnects the missing piece, and delivers the construction all repaired and ready for audition. Here, it's . . . I meant to say.

Ted, who's let Dirk and our thirty-year-old take the first steps into the shallow end of this nascent conversation, contemplating it all with a sort of didactic benevolence, now joins in, diving dolphin-like, hop, hop, maneuvering in perfect form, his movements scalloping expanses of water that stir up lacy edges around him.

Shivering in their towels, their feet on damp tiles—so propitious for the culture of the microscopic fungal elements that cover its surface that they leave the sole of the foot with the sensation of some sticky, downy felt—the two others admire his harmonious movements from the edge of the pool, his movements in that aqueous milieu which he stirs like silky cotton (and not the stuff that's always a bit too cold, that stings your eyes, that always leaves an unpleasant taste on your tongue and seems unable to carry your weight). Still, every now and again, they both let their admiration pause for a moment so their minds can flit off to something else.

Dirk, for example, once or twice in the course of their conversation, removes his boot (this operation is apparently not self-explanatory but demands efforts so far-reaching that they even tug on his facial muscles) so as to massage his foot through its sock, steadily, conscientiously and—we're going to say—with not even a hint of neurosis.

Usually the end result of this project is simply the extra comfort procured by the action of expert fingers bringing the circulation back into muscles or nerves, except, wait, this time there's something there, something annoying him, and he doesn't really know what, so we have to elucidate.

This intruder, very small in stature and essentially unknown (is it, let's see, a crumb, a pebble, a bit of paper that stuck to his foot when he got out of bed, some kind of peeling, a flake that came off some vaster entity?), having infiltrated between the stitches of the sock-wool, has slid between the sole of Dirk's foot and this selfsame wool—anyway, that's a possibility—having profited from a moment's inattention perhaps, or, having settled into the hollow of his bare foot, hiding there until the sock came to ensure that it would stay put, gluing it tightly to the cutaneous layer. Be that as it may, however, this intruder, which up till now had lain dormant, without demanding attention, has suddenly become the source of a vague irritation, and Dirk is now going so far as to remove the sock itself, which, inside out and crunched up into a shape that's, what, somewhat conical, doesn't look like much: no longer simulating, as it did when opened up and properly unfolded, the morphology of the foot, no longer brandishing this simulacrum in the space of the courtyard, having entirely lost the appearance of an excellent envelope for the aforementioned limb, having lost even the slightest remaining representational aspect that might cause us to look kindly upon the rough and abstract ball that Dirk now drops on the ground in order to get a better look at the arch of his foot—which, however, seems intact as far as the presence of any possible UFO stuck there is concerned.

This arch (and patient examination seems not to refute this fact) is completely depopulated, somewhat blackened, really, marked with a few craters or depressions here and there where the imprint of a hostile but already ancient piece of gravel, the tip of a flint, or even a breadcrumb had, laid sideways, made a good cut, or else indicating where a stray splinter had drilled in, or who knows what else, years ago now, these abrasions having fossilized into a personal diary of dangers weathered, a host of proofs recorded there in his skin of the inherent dangers of venturing out of bed—but, otherwise, fine, nothing significant, no foreign bodies, nothing at all.

Dirk dusts himself off anyhow with the palm of his hand: not one single heterogeneous element comes to light or flakes off, neither falling in a dull shower down to earth nor dropping to the ground as a single piece, nor—Dirk brings his palm up to eye level and studies it attentively—remaining in the cup of his hand.

Then Dirk's upper lip, instantly followed in this action by the lower, which sticks to it with the adhesive strength of a shellfish on the rocky surface where it's chosen to make its home, juts out in a doubtful pout meant for himself alone.

I'm insisting on the private nature of this expression because, in this case, it is in no way intended to call the attention of the two other men to the subject of Dirk's questionable situation and how deprived his almost fruitless search has left him; he is making absolutely no attempt to alert them by means of his expression, an expression that (in another context, and had they misunderstood the meaning of this pout) might have distracted them from the flow of the conversation that they are conducting, good for them, at an excellent pace.

Far from wishing to interrupt them to solicit their support in this minor, really rather private affair, it's more to keep maintaining contact with himself that Dirk puts his lips together in this explicit manner, to convince himself that he is paying attention to what he does, a silent way of saying, Yes, yes, Dirk, it's clear to me that you took your sock off to get rid of the intruder and that you see absolutely no intruder, and I acknowledge that this is a very strange thing—thus addressing his pout to the other portion of himself, the portion that just did all this work and yet is making no progress in its search, indicating to this detective that he shares its perplexity and is likewise setting his own interpretive faculties in motion with nothing but good will but no more success, experiencing the same doubt, and, in the end, after a long process of reflection, tacitly agreeing with it and choosing to suspend the search. Let's just see what's in store for us next, the two detectives tell each other, hands in the pockets of their trench coats, walking off together into the distance, seen from behind, down the converging lines of the main road.

This pout, reflecting, therefore, the cooperation between Dirk's other self and the first one, and initiating the aforementioned, if brief, interior dialogue, is soon succeeded by a more turbulent movement wherein Dirk's forehead is suddenly invaded by a pattern of superimposed, ingrained wavelets, depicting— given his ongoing amazement at not having found the guilty article—the justified fear that, once he has restored first the wooly and then the sturdy foot-protection systems to their proper place, the sensation will still be there, since he has not been able to eradicate the cause.

These wavelets are no longer a sign made by one of his selves, full of solicitude for another, but are rather—as those two selves reunite now and fuse completely—the involuntary trace of an almost total absence from the general conversational situation in which Dirk is, nonetheless, immersed.

This freely unfurling swell, soon covering the entire frontal surface of Dirk Lange's face, is evidence of the fact that, while there may be two men in this trio who are present in both body and mind (and even then, these minds, of course, might themselves be tempted to take the sort of subsidiary paths that absolutely everybody permits himself in collective situations—nothing very serious: only fictional characters are completely wrapped up in what they are doing), the third, however, is present only in body, his mind having totally abdicated in order to throw itself into its silent anxiety, leaving the other two to carry on without it.

Since Dirk's disquiet has spread outside the bounds of any language, it doesn't even take the form of a parallel monologue where, the local inquiry having failed, he might attempt, rationally and through abstract reasoning, to give a name to the element responsible for this physical annoyance. Instead, it undulates, this disquiet, in the depths of silence, as if his mind, yes, wearing swim fins and zipped into a waterproof suit, were diving into deep waters, down where the celestial light no longer reaches, with just a small lamp hooked, we can imagine it, onto the band holding his mask to his head, and following, in this manner, with a constant flutter of his ankles, the weak beam of light with which this lamp saws through the aquatic mass, to single out, here and there, a few flat beds of seaweed, a few stones pitted with every kind of cavity, a school of rather placid fish in whose brains there probably isn't much in the way of thought either, and the muddy sand, stretching out for miles, mixed with all sorts of vegetable and animal elements that, as they decompose, are producing a dark sediment that stretches on in long, blackish, olive-colored patches occasionally traversed by a reddish, flickering glint.

3

Now, what is the subject of this conversation that each conducts in his own way, in the manner just described? It concerns a brawl that, just yesterday evening, had pitted two locals against each other, residents whom you hadn't met when we left the porch on our way to the ranch, for the very good reason that one of them was still in bed on the first floor of one of the houses we went by (one, two, three—I'd say the fourth one from the inn), doing mighty poorly in fact, moaning and groaning in his bedroom, while the other, thinking it pointless to display his black eye unnecessarily, with the swollen bruise forming welts like sizzling butter on his skin, had sunk his silhouette into the background darkness of his room when he heard the footsteps of our thirty-year-old coming perilously close to the rectangle of his window (plus your footsteps and my own, both of us looking like Spencer Tracy in *Bad Day at Black Rock*—sticking out in our city clothes in all this western scenery), trying to hide the lingering proof of his lack of foresight regarding that underhanded left hook—a left hook that had landed when, objectively, one would have been perfectly justified in expecting a right . . . in my opinion at least.

The first of these two men is named Howard Nelson, the second Richard Evans.

Howard, if you're up for a biography—a quick sketch, really, because the facts at my disposal aren't exactly legion—got here maybe ten years ago driving a makeshift truck into which he'd crammed a chest of drawers made from curly maple, an oil painting, and two or three changes of clothing. He, along with some others, then worked together to construct his house so that afterwards he could place, in the room allotted to him, that is, "Harry's Place"—in addition to a homemade table with an adjoining bench and two or three bits and pieces bought from the General Store—this same chest of drawers and above it this same painting, these being the only evidence that, like anyone else, he had a past.

As far as telling what the content of this past might be, the only way to guess at it would be to sit on his bench and contemplate the painting for a long time in the hope that it might deliver a brief version of it. A stone house covered with the abundant blooms of a climbing rose with a delicate honeycomb of foliage and stems that have neglected no opportunity to perform arabesques, sitting imposingly in the middle of a meadow whose grass had become somewhat faded over the years. No matter how hard you look, identifying a hazelnut or a filbert among the trees hedging the garden, in front of the thick splotches of the hills with crests that vanish beneath the overwhelming weight of a low, overcast sky, locating, without much conviction, a prepubescent maple whose scarce, palmate foliage has sunk so deeply beneath the painting's varnish that you have to pay very close attention to find the purple pigments in it, your gaze always comes up against the opaque windowpanes where two white strokes indicate a reflection, and the closed door topped by a bull's-eye window behind which a short, yellow curtain is drawn.

It may be that—rather than inspecting, more or less scrupulously, the painting—if you crouched down next to the chest of drawers to listen to the tale it had to tell, you might have figured out a bit more. Because it was perfectly ready to come out of the shadows, revealing its own story as well as giving evidence of its owner's. Temperamentally loquacious, and as capable as any other witness, it wouldn't have balked at indulging in a brief prosopopoeia. It could, for instance, have proceeded by means of its various lesions, inviting deductions as to their chronology, but then also by means of its manner of construction, by the label (yellowed, but still legible) that indicates its provenance, by the wallpaper (faded—but blossoms of blue and mauve still bloom on it against a background of sea-green foliage) lining the bottom of its drawers (and tacked there by someone or other—a glimpse of whose identity the wallpaper itself, perhaps, might have revealed), and even more by the objects contained in its compartments and that it had transported, hidden from sight, in the truck that first brought it here. But we'd be embarrassed to go digging around in other people's drawers, wouldn't we, so we'll leave it at that.

As for Richard Evans: he takes part in every drinking spree in town, has an obviously volatile temperament, and sports a moustache that constantly hesitates—decisions, decisions— between a strong brown and a more temperate blond, endowed with hairs of both colors engaged in a merciless battle for priority on his upper lip. Sometimes you'd swear the brown ones are winning, sometimes the blond ones, and sometimes it's an inextricable free-for-all making a final verdict impossible. It's clear that this conflict must represent the hairy equivalent of the same contradictory impulses that do battle in Richard's mind. His wild eyes, caught between these two independent battles—on the upper level, his conflicting ideas smashing into each other, and, on the lower, the aforementioned, heterogeneous, tyrannical pilosity; each case, above and below, representative of one particular color's struggle to impose itself on another—conscious of such omnipresent danger, direct a ferocious gaze at anything and everything.

We can glean from the beginnings of Dirk, Ted, and our thirty-year-old's conversation that Richard and Howard had each arrived from his own direction to lean their elbows on the bar along with some other men whose particulars might be provided if they had a personal part to play in our story, but who are merely present to make up a credible crowd for an evening in a saloon.

They ordered some whiskeys, each one at his own pace at first, and then drinks all around paid for by one or the other. This game of rounds, originating in a generous impulse, quickly became the occasion for a sort of rivalry in which, with each order, the contestants' eyes would meet and clash.

They continued this ophthalmic duel for a bit. Their gazes challenged each other defiantly from one end of the bar to the other, sending off microscopic carrier pigeons through the black apertures of their pupils, these birds charging toward the equally spherical and dilated apertures of the enemy, plunging in to leave behind a mean little note scrawled with awkward insults.

Then each duelist must have asked himself whether or not he would proceed farther than this ocular stichomythia. A second phase in which sharp words would be convoked might very well lead to a third stage defined by a more physical response. From each side of the bar, Howard Nelson and Richard Evans weighed the pros and cons of this scenario for themselves, taking no more and no less time than was necessary.

Let's take a closer look at just what it was that Howard and Richard were engaged in weighing, deep down inside.

As far as the pros: well, it would be a source of free amusement for other men in the bar, the kind of social sacrifice that it's sometimes good to be able to make, and one that would ever-so-slightly relieve their own boredom with all the recent, peaceful, monotonous evenings.

As far as the cons: the prospect of a sleepless night, window open onto the old moon laid out as usual in its sky. Because contusions don't take naps, never stop reminding you that they're there, blathering on endlessly in little bursts of ego, constantly demanding that you remember them, staying awake to rob you of sleep.

In the opening of rhetorical hostilities, who went first? Whoever went second, since it had come to this, leapt bravely and immediately into the breach. The combatants proceeded gradually, exactly as custom dictates, raising the pitch with each retort—really, from the point of view of the norms current to the period under discussion, everything went ahead very acceptably.

The verbiage passing back and forth over the bar between the two men simultaneously expressed and further incited their anger, each phrase fired off setting its speaker free of an excess of annoyance while conversely swelling the other's instantly revived irritation. This dispute had quickened the vascularization of both their faces, which began to turn red, a rather subtle red at first, and then brighter and brighter, almost a strawberry red, followed by other physical symptoms, a sensation of heat, sweating, a feeling of swelling, particularly at chest level, as if this anger had lived there for ages like some kind of animal, a tame and manageable creature that used to sleep there without their worrying about it, that they carried around like a parasite wherever they went, but that now, deciding to wake up, was growing, becoming more and more enormous, pressing against their gastric walls, compressing their lungs, beginning to slip a tentacle this way and that, until finally it became absolutely urgent to let the creature out, it having, in any event, begun to do everything in its power to clear itself a path—one of its tentacles speckled with hideous suckers all but emerging from one of their nostrils, twisting itself horribly in the air, yuck—in the end, something had to be done, and fast. So, finally, they took their feud outside, shoulder to shoulder, surrounded by all the others, their rambling haste raising a single cloud of dust as they both proceeded into the dirt yard behind the saloon.

The fight, fine, you know what those are like, two men (having removed their jackets and tossed them like footballs to one or another of the extras who then held it to his belly as obstinately as if he were going to run and set it down behind the goal line) confront each other outside in the dark, grapple hand-to-hand in a crumple of skin and fiber.

The glare coming from the back window of the saloon splashes across their shirts, splatters onto their faces, lights up a cheek where sweat reflects it to perfection, bounces nicely off the clean cotton of a shoulder, or of a leg attempting to complete a scissor hold in the arena, onto the enamel of a tooth—crack!—into the white of an eye, spurting better yet onto a silver button, the hook of some overalls, before finally going opaque, dulled by the dirt gradually covering the fighters, these men who roll on the ground, get up as best they can, fall again—soon just two chthonian creatures created from the same dark mud to which they constantly return.

Dirk, stricken by an onychophagic impulse, nibbles on the horny extremity of his index finger, while Ted and our thirty-year-old discuss the various martial arts and dirty tricks deployed by Richard and Howard: all the uppercuts, hooks, and jabs to the accompaniment of gleeful shouts from the spectators, one or two improvised holds, take this! a fast one, and there you go, I'm trying to pin one of your arms behind your back, but the other arm still has some fight in it. And when they fall down together, the luminous rectangle cast by the saloon window shatters along with their petty egos.

Among the spectators who crowded around the two men and who stared wide-eyed at the fight in an attempt to make sense of its progress—which, in spite of everything, seemed to be represented by nothing more than abstract flashes of light and shadow tossing and turning angrily in bursts of sparks and flecks, in the middle of a circus ring whose undulating circumference, defined by their gathering, retracted whenever the two men fell to the ground and then opened wider whenever they got back up again—our three energumens, distributed at different points of the fluctuating external limit of this circle, had differing assessments of what exactly went on. Ted, apparently, had been most involved with the scene. Sometimes he would interject a few shouts of approval, which, launched into the air, had some difficulty locating the tympanum of the man being praised, who, from where he was embroiled in the twists and turns of battle and suffering various collisions with the earth, imagined more than heard these guttural, panegyric scraps. Sometimes too Ted would spit and splutter a few words of contempt that slunk off to die in the sand: little translucent toads reflecting a final flash of light under a feeble moonbeam before being sucked back into the earth.

Remember how much you liked it, Ted, last night's fight? You were one of the most forceful initiators of the movements of the cordon formed by us spectators, retracting or extending as necessary, says, in substance, our thirty-year-old, whereas we ourselves always lagged a little behind, sometimes getting our feet caught up in the movement, sometimes stamping against the tide because of being so unprepared for the speed of it all. You made every kind of gesture to urge them on, he says, lingering over the sight of Ted gesticulating at the edge of the fight—using a peculiar kind of manual alphabet, probably spontaneously understood by all concerned at the time, but obscure in its choices even now . . .

Because, if you think about it, from the point of view of a linguist, of course, as regards the ideograms traced in the air by Ted's waving hands and fingers in the flickering light of the scuffle, it's been universally agreed that you have to give up on seeing these as analogical in any way—i.e., the hands representing, as realistically as possible, the objects, ideas, feelings, or actions to which they referred. No, it's best to opt for a more arbitrary kind of construction, bearing no relationship of resemblance—even a tenuous one—between the shape of each of his hands or their respective positions in space and the semantic content whose vehicle they had become.

A puppeteer's hands, really, because you seemed to be pulling the strings in this fight, working Howard's body from a distance, picking it up when necessary, sending it back in Richard's direction—you had to be fair, but it was still Howard's side you were on, having publicly bet a few dollars on the Howard's favor. You acknowledged that Rich wasn't doing so badly, you were a good sport as usual, but Howard was your protégé and you kept on going in the night air, directing your man the best you could by means of your puppeteer's hands.

Ted has no trouble imagining what our thirty-year-old recounts to him. From the entire series of uppercuts that they were present to witness, he now chooses one—the acme, in his opinion, the high point, I'd say, of the fighting, the moment when, really, well, a good shot, right? He turns some of it over in detail like dirt being plowed, like dough being worked.

Abandoning the nail now in favor of skin, despite this being more tender, chewing rather relentlessly into his digital pulp, Dirk has abandoned thoughts of resorting once more to his full arsenal of chains, hooks, etc., and just, from time to time, so as to pretend he's participating in the collective account, at least by agreeing, nods Yes, inwardly thanking his sternocleidomastoid muscles for so willingly transmitting his (apparent) acquiescence.

Out of politeness, our thirty-year-old gives his opinion in turn, without being sure he knows which uppercut is being discussed, perfectly happy with an approximate understanding, because, between you and me, he himself now feels the need to pull back a little from the conversation to which he considers he has already made the proper contribution, so as to attend to a few of his own thoughts, whose thread he will follow halfheartedly, at a leisurely pace, since nobody's going to check up on him, conceiving a few, poor, skinny little subjects about the size of marbles, hard as flint, into which he'll flick a shooter from time to time, watching them scatter and then roll around on the rocky, deserted surface of his mind.

That being said, the narrative of the fight is going to jump around a bit.

For example, when our thirty-year-old slices rather unpredictably into a brief silence with the blade of a remark nobody saw coming, redirecting their various minds and causing these to converge on a certain Mr. last name Evans, first name Richard, to whom they'd all given short shrift earlier, at least from his point of view.

There follows a number of corrections, attempts to put things in balance, our man indulging at will in fabricating a few pronouncements relating to Rich Evans, thus hoping to get things going. But for Ted, Howard's superiority is never really in question. You can talk about Rich if you want to, but no matter what you say, Howard will always come out on top, it's a matter of technique.

Dirk doesn't participate. Letting himself be carried along by an eastern breeze (our thirty-year-old is sitting to his right) and then one from the west (Ted is there on his left) with the placid submission of a weather vane, his thoughts go to Rich, his indecisive moustache, his skin's excessive vascularization, his dark irises that seem to merge into his pupils; then to Howard, to the story of his arrival in that truck, a story heard so many times at the gaming table in the saloon, to Howard's furniture come from who knows where, to the painting that they say hangs facing his bed and the painted vegetation there he must submerge his eyes in every night and every morning, with the same nostalgic and futile constancy.

Dirk plunges back into his deep waters.

The tip of his index finger, well done! now bristles with hangnails dangling like tiny translucent pennants, a bit pale and vaguely cellulous.

Once again he briefly surveys his watery depths as they reveal themselves in the slim beam of his headlamp. How many minutes does he let go by before thinking that maybe it's time to return responsibly to the surface? A huge muscular effort. Undulations and swaying hips. This done, he notices that on the surface things have, yes, changed somewhat.

4

Ted and our thirty-year-old, still sitting there, have arrived at a serene silence, from which, using it to its best advantage, they've each taken a little dive of their own; oh, nothing very ambitious, only as far down as where the sunshine still allows one to see safely into the shallow depths, and all you need is a snorkel.

They splash around, grasping through their masks' poor glass the almost unadorned, dull ochre sand, nothing much in the way of seashells, watching a bit of stray seaweed almost sway into the picture, but really there's almost nothing to see, while their bare feet beat somewhat phlegmatically against the mass of the water.

For a while, Dirk contemplates the two short, black sticks moving around on the marine dermis like two mobile splinters, and then—is it because they feel they're being watched?—the snorkel-connected divers surface again.

Snorting, emptying their leaky masks, breathing into their snorkels to get any drops of water out, they return to the courtyard, meet Dirk's gaze, are delighted to see his eyes sharp again and his forehead now unclouded, and, contact having been resumed, all parties are now ready for new conversational adventures.

Ted picks up the torch alone.

His tale is like a salve to them, it moves over their minds like, yes, like a balm after the solitude in which they've all been maneuvering for a time, down in the inmost depths of the marine caverns from which they've now emerged, speleologists somewhat pained by this harsh reunion with the light (hence their appreciation of Ted's soothing anecdote).

The episode in question took place just this morning, you're the first to hear it, it's a story of dawn, Ted tells them, you have to imagine the liminal state of the light, the slow emergence of day synchronized with a likewise emerging consciousness. His audience have no difficulty picturing the corral bathed in this atmosphere of beginning, where Ted explains how, after coming down from his room, he leaned with his back against the post, the same one on which, when there's occasion for a siesta, Dirk attaches the hook of his hammock, still dangling—suspended at present by a single nail—like a big albino bat blinded by the sun.

It had been a hard night, something in the air wasn't right. The daytime temperature had persisted in his room, but a cold breeze had blown through the window, battling this suspended warmth, digging little invisible, zigzag tunnels—mottling and streaking the room—into the slightly heavy gaseous matter it encountered.

Maybe because this surrounding belligerence ended up having some effect on our candidate for sleep, the annoyance experienced by the intruding air being something contagious, perhaps—likewise felt by the inside-air that had expected to reign, utterly stagnant, in the room throughout the night—in any case, Ted failed miserably, rotation after rotation, in achieving what he sought, his body ending up entangled in his cotton sheet, which soon turned into a trap, a net closing over the creature it had caught, stupidly thrashing around in its mesh.

Caught in the crossfire between the cold breeze, whose acid arrowheads, whose various drills and trepans busied themselves in any number of points on his body, and then the heat resisting it (and since the air coming in from outside dragged some of its, who knows, somewhat enervating vegetal essences along with it), Ted (though, actually, maybe he really did sleep, but without noticing he did so, the way we sometimes lie there on our beds thinking we're awake from start to finish whereas the truth is, unknowingly, we gave in to sleep in dreamlike segments too atonic to be remembered, or which, sly things, consisted precisely in making us dream that we couldn't get to sleep) put an end to his torture by leaving his room to go out and muse in the delicate colorings of dawn—a pleasant enough thing, once in a while, to be immersed in.

So it was there, leaning against the aforesaid post, drawing the landscape in through the slits between his eyelids—still rather indistinct, but revealing itself with perceptible velocity, like a landscape drawn in invisible ink that you've now placed in front of a heat source (which isn't far from the truth, if you think about it)—that Ted began to let his thoughts go wherever they wanted, superimposing on the dim corral what he recalled of the series of futile positions he had tested in order to ward off his insomnia, sometimes perfect symmetries, for example taking the shape of an airplane, legs close together in a good imitation of fuselage, arms open at a slight angle on either side, almost aerodynamic, asking nothing more than to enter the airy, celestial, nebulous spheres of sleep; sometimes in arrangements that were a little more expressionist, a bent arm, a hip obviously out of line, one wrist excrescent, one hand crooked; but nothing worked, as far as this gymnastic obstinacy, neither (methodically), lying flat on his stomach, looking like someone panning for gold while lying on the bank of a stream, you know what I mean, sort of stretching his sieve out over the water without collecting a single nugget of gold; nor on his side, a bit like a gundog; nor on his back, spread-eagled and staring up at the ceiling like a shepherd looking at the starry sky above; and, each time, his face seeking out another position for itself, buried in the striped cloth of the mattress like an ostrich in its desert, or resting sideways, mouth sagging slightly, as if drawn freehand, erased by the tip of a finger here and there, merging with the sheet spread out all around it, or else completely face up, presented in a sort of pre-death mask where the entire foreshortened body looks like the subject of one of those paintings done in a medical amphitheater, let's break off the comparison there; anyhow, Ted, the one telling this story (did he mime the positions he described, the bestiary he convoked, the anxious haste of his gold prospector?), Ted, who, leaning against his post, felt the charm of dawn gradually come over him and be substituted for his waning annoyance, noticed *goddamn*, as the contours of the cattle became clear, separating into autonomous units, one, two, three, four . . . eight, *well I'll be damned!* (does that sound authentic?) one cow was missing.

Adrenalin successfully eliminating by its extremely radical means the diffuse sluggishness and physical reticence that his body, still numbed by its bad night, would otherwise have had to fight off on its own, Ted grabs his lasso and leaps bareback onto one of the three chestnuts that thought they were still going to have a couple of peaceful hours of sleep that morning.

Making an immediate, intuitive selection, he chooses one of the several equiprobable directions, and heads off hell for leather toward the background scenery that is still thank God turning yellow and becoming clearer with each equine stride.

Just as a fisherman thinks he understands the piscatorial psychology of his prey, boldly imputing character traits to his quarry, knowing its flaws, its weaknesses, what might make it susceptible to being caught unawares, guessing its preferences and, with the greatest sincerity—he would almost stake his life on it—drawing conclusions from these penchants, his eye focused on the fluid surface of the river and his mind happy at the prospect of the necessary sequence of causes and effects that he is preparing to witness, Ted, likewise, has no trouble with putting himself in the place of the bovid he is chasing.

It was back in the dark of night when the bovid heard the erratic banging of the gate, the braided cord ordinarily keeping it shut apparently having come loose and letting out a little more slack with every new reverberation. The other artiodactyl mammals are asleep, but this one has its ear—the only part moving, as it hasn't yet bothered to move the rest of its carcass as yet, lying on the sand—pricked, aimed at interpreting this sound. The live, breaking news of the strap's progress towards coming untied surges into this ear. The animal doesn't get up until the time is right, not wanting to risk any useless commotion that might wake the other cows up. It waits, forces itself to stay awake with the help of the anemic moonbeam falling near the hills off in the distance. Flocks of gray clouds play peekaboo in front of the round, white heavenly body. Using what mnemic means it has at its disposal, our bovid remembers that it has not always been confined inside these fences. From this sonorous rhythm, so sweet to its ear—because holding out a hope it could no longer really conceive of, since, for ages now, it has lived the hours of its life as they came, forcing itself not to think about anything—it gathers up the buried images of nourishing summer pastures, it sees again the mountains' vast decorative abundance. And the water in rivers, it was about to forget the river water where it could noisily quench its thirst, while the cowboys, without getting down from their mounts, dipped their hats into the surface of the water, yes, took their hats off just like that and swung their open Stetsons like bowls onto the skin of the water, swept them over it, their horses submerged halfway up their legs, collecting the ever-escaping water, a great deal of which fell back along the soft, impractical edges of their improvised cups as they lifted them to their lips.

The strap holding the gate had now completely slipped off. Giving one last thought to the human who tended it, our bovine said a brief mental goodbye to Ted and, finally getting up, left via the half-open gate.

Ted keeps galloping headlong toward the hills through which they had first come to this town with their herds.

Dawn's exhaustive attentions scrub clean the land still blackened by the previous hours. Benefiting from this increased visibility, Ted's eyes begin searching the countryside. The bovid, our psychologist-cowboy says to himself, after setting out with wild, delighted strides, must have adopted a slower rhythm, meaning it stopped to rest here and there to contemplate with its nyctalopic gaze the infinite reach of nature spread out around it.

All these rest stops mean it can't be too far away now.

Soon this hypothesis finds itself reinforced by the existence of some half-eaten underbrush, the ingestion of which—I take this wet sap as proof—appears recent; though there's not much, it's still shiny: not quite healed over.

Ted slows down to trot along the rocky stretches flooding with morning light in a continuous lateral stream, so that only half of each element—scrub-brush, pebble, the rare grove of cacti—is revealed, the other side preferring to remain hidden in a kind of nocturnal ignorance.

What did I tell you! There it is, our prodigal bovid, sniffing at the ground near some large-paddled prickly pears.

It lifts its grim eye toward Ted and takes in the horrible image of his silhouette making its imprint in the landscape in a manner known to it alone, since it doesn't see the same way we do (there have been numerous studies on the subject). At first tetanized by this apparition, one perhaps it hadn't expected, having been completely occupied by looking for a bit of edible vegetation in this rocky mess, and also pretty groggy from its expedition, it makes an attempt at escaping, but without much conviction, knowing who's boss and having few illusions on the subject of the brief run it performs, above all for the sake of appearances.

It takes off heavily through the stones, permits itself to screech around a corner behind a clump of cacti, complicates the chase with some nonetheless purely conventional dodges and feints, while, prettily spinning his lasso in the now-bright sky of this brand-new morning, Ted gallops after.

The pursued and the pursuer continue to play their roles and then, there you have it, the white, misshapen oval of the rope begins twirling like an upside-down map delineating over the massive body of the poor animal the contours of a lake in which you could almost drown.

The dreadful circumference of this outlined water keeps on shifting, increasing the vertigo of our bovid as it skims over this upside-down landscape. This rather fascinating optical effect causes its hooves to become slightly confused. Its brain, troubled by the false landscape—not exactly in the habit of being airborne—and literally flabbergasted by its lacustrine mobility, is no longer sending entirely correct orders to nerves and muscles, which introduces a most distressing disorder into its locomotive system.

It's a sure thing, if it keeps on like this, it's on the road to ruin, it's going to fall, it falls, the lake becomes a large pond, the pond shrinks, becomes just a fishing hole, and then what? a mere puddle slightly larger than the animal's body at first, then the same proportions, maybe a bit narrower because now it's squeezing it a little, yes, the rope is around it, stops it in its mad dash, makes it fall down on the ground where it slides for a while, getting really and truly dusty.

Come on, says Ted, this little game of runaway is over. And the other, choking back its humiliation, tries hard to be reasonable on their way back, turning the situation to its advantage, transforming in its mind this man who tows it by a rope through the vast stretches of dry, almost waxy ochre into its valet, whose business it is, after all, to provide it with meals, telling itself so successfully that it's going back to be with its comrades again, *e tutti quanti*, as my ancestors used to say, that, rolling around in its mind the malleable bubble of its remembered escapade, it makes, all in all, a pretty serene homecoming.

5

This more or less happy conclusion to an affair that might have gone considerably worse coincides with the arrival of Mary.

Okay, Mary: slender, almost ethereal silhouette, in a baize dress where your sharp eye spots percaline cuffs introducing—where all else is dull and matte—two glistening bands that move as her hands move, a straw hat tied on with a bright blue ribbon, carrying a basket of provisions firmly settled into the crook of her arm, officially listed as the sole employee of the sole improvised cleaning establishment the backyard of which is used for drying the laundry that, with all its different figures in random coloration, hides fragments of the landscape of desert hills spread out beyond.

Mary's arrival changes the atmosphere considerably. Red checkered napkins to be spread out on a table, the oval presence of the willow basket with its top divided into two bucolic flaps, reminding you of old family picnics buried deep in your prehistory because it's the perfect incarnation of the very notion of a simple, organized, yet nomadic meal in the countryside and what that used to consist of—and, associating their functions, nothing excludes your summoning up the plastic cooler your parents might have brought along as well. Are you thinking of those high, sandy spots where wooden tables had been set out on the ground by provident municipalities in order to point out the already-discovered spots affording the best views, while you yourself were strewing bits of animal and vegetable stuff about and contemplating the comings and goings of the tide, and half-heartedly, awaiting the moment you'd be able to ford your way over to the nearby island; or, rather, are you thinking of highway rest stops, the concrete structures under which your numb and naked legs would fold up, while, a few steps away, the driver stretched his sore muscles in vaguely gymnastic movements punctuated from time to time with loud exhalations resembling a singsong tone more indicative of some sort of physical satisfaction than of breath expelled through exertion, while, again, you, being less happy than he, got a slap on the back of the hand that had started digging around in the sandwiches brought along, all wrapped up, the sandwiches whose contents, when you were finally given one, you examined suspiciously, lifting the top slice of bread that, softened by contact with the damp contents, had acquired a flexible texture, making inspection easy and then, sometimes, as a consequence of this suspicious examination, when another child was present on the scene (whether his presence can be explained on congenital grounds or biographically, your having been able to make some friends at school), negotiating an exchange based either—you didn't know which—on genuine preferences or rather on the confused feeling that you were never given what actually suited you while other people got exactly what they wanted. And, as for me, this would have been in the fields with the little baby blue Simca parked nearby, the one that leaked water (an infirmity that made for segmented trips since it was necessary to stop regularly to fill up the radiator), and I no longer know if we were sitting on the grass (were there a few chairs that we used to unfold stuffed somehow into the too narrow trunk?—I can't quite picture a roof-rack—maybe just a single folding chair, shoved in however it would fit, reserved for old Yvonne who, actually, was sweet and young and a little stout, in her print knit dresses with the lace of a nylon slip sticking out from underneath when she sat in the hypothetical folding chair), in the midst of members of the ant family and dried grasses—you could always pick a stalk and stick it in your mouth and do some thinking; that's something I used to like to do a lot as a child, having moreover a secret proclivity for chewing on rose petals too, after a neighbor—over for drinks while I must have been hovering around the group under the parasol with its big white fringe and sucking on some peanuts that I couldn't get myself to like—proclaimed them edible as well as the natural accompaniment for I don't know what dish, as were the few, crumpled nasturtiums planted in the garden at the foot of some apple trees, and for which, for this same reason, and alas for them, I reserved the same fate; also, I'm back to our picnic, in the midst of buttercups and the *Leontodon taraxacum* that we never called anything but dandelions—as far as I can remember, their flowers a just-slightly-darker yellow and their dehiscent fruits displaying a bundle of silk in beautiful, precarious, vulnerable, labile bubbles whose feathered achenes scattered at the least breath; and adult voices moved around testing out new phrases in the rustic air, lungs inflating better here, but occasionally stymied nevertheless by surprise gusts of wind blowing the sound of certain phonemes back to them, giving their speech a different modulation than it had in the city. Beneath the foliage, the head of the thermos of coffee they'd go retrieve later on—with its one fat ear—was visible via the open trunk of the car.

As for our characters, there they are, eating with their fingers, the food having been divided up onto napkins, gnawing on the dried meat, tearing the brown bread apart, and a little later removing the stem from a cherry and then picking up a neighboring fruit.

It's Ted, generous man, who in conversational fragments much less structured than those that came earlier, utilizing those sorts of tiny islands that one inserts in the interstices of chewing, a matter of keeping in touch, a subtle contact needing no more than these intermittent manifestations, the very fact of chewing at the same time and in the same place being already, you now realize, a way—albeit partial—of being together, who recalls, as if in passing, look! the maple grove, the one where he lived a few years back, the lobed and stalked foliage softly waving against the skies.

Ted pauses briefly in his chewing, which lets his audience imagine the branches waving in the wind, not too long a masticatory pause, however, perhaps to ensure that none of the men at the table takes advantage of the vacuum to bring up a new subject; then Ted moves right on to the cabin where they used to distill syrup and the others imagine the log walls, in their minds they enter the room's darkness, examine the equipment, lightly rub a hand on a work surface, turn something mysterious over to see how it might work, and Ted, having swallowed completely, soon starts in on a more technical explanation of how you bore holes in the trunks; at that point they go back outdoors into the brisk air, they watch how he does it, see with satisfaction the flowing sap, while the food they themselves are ingesting begins, why hide the fact, to take on an agreeable weight in their stomach sacs.

Ted takes an additional mouthful, swallows it almost as is, hardly calling on his grinding faculties at all, so as to regain as quickly as possible the instruments of his linguistic function and there they all go back into the cabin with him. In one nook, vented by a shaft opening onto the gray sky, is the kettle in which the substance that interests them all is boiling, and which, Ted warns them as he ingurgitates a final tiny morsel that he impregnates in passing, while continuing to talk, with saliva (a digestive aid in itself, thanks to the function performed by ptyalin, so that it isn't actually always necessary to resort to the use of teeth), has to be stirred later, and I think I've told you everything there is to know about this technique.

The others approve, give thanks implicitly, experience a sort of overall contentment regarding Ted, the food whose beneficial elements, vitamins, proteins, various sugars, I don't know what else, are progressively having their effect, spreading a new, slow-moving strength throughout their bodies, one that is simultaneously an exquisite laziness and, ultimately, considering the present moment in general, one that is, well, not at all disagreeable, far from it.

At this point Mary offers to make coffee.

To that end, followed by Dirk, on the grounds of giving her a hand, she goes into the house. From the courtyard terrace you can't really tell exactly what's going on inside the house during this optional scene between Dirk and Mary, who are probably handling cups and saucers, putting them on a tray of course, heating up some water while Dirk, perhaps, rather than Mary, grinds the coffee, since the handle gets easily jammed, I'll do it, he might have suggested, while in the dark interior we can place a cupboard as well as a clock imprisoned in its wooden case.

I leave the finishing touches to you.

Anyhow, Mary comes back out carrying the tea set on its tray and brushing against Dirk who was already standing in the doorway. Our four individuals stir their spoons in the china, having returned to their own thoughts, making the little clinking sound that is characteristic of the end of meals. Dirk is very dreamy. What, exactly, happened in the kitchen?

The solitude of this reverie goes on for a bit, each man letting his attention wander off to lands about which no travel journal could ever really be written. Having the sense that this separation of his comrades' minds from one another as they each secretly follow differing paths into the spongy kind of thought secreted by digestion is growing more pronounced, Ted, always the unifier, picks up his guitar. And now, tintintintin, rantamplan, rantamplan, drumroll, cut to a close-up, and here's Ted getting ready to play us a little song.

Leaning against the wall in a corner of the courtyard, the aforementioned guitar had occasionally been visited in its hours of isolation by some saurian setting its cautious feet on its frets and avoiding, one by one, the possibilities of stumbling presented by each of its strings. More often than not the gecko would very quickly turn upside down with a lacertilian switch of its hips, fearing that, if it fell through the round hole, it would be caught in the resonance chamber and there hurl itself thousands of times against the walls, panicked between the patches of darkness and the shaft letting in the daylight. And even though it's possible to venture the hypothesis that it, in this instance, would be able to demonstrate more resourcefulness than the various wasps I've met, who when caught in the makeshift trap of a plastic bottle with its neck shoved in backwards between its walls, fly around stupidly, hedgehopping over the field of jam where they would get their feet caught and be destined to stick there and die, wandering endlessly around above this bait without ever locating the exit, a small disk of sky with a circumference probably too narrow for them to notice, especially where it is, far inside the bottle, from their perspective (a memory dating back to a point only slightly more recent than my picnic, and I don't know where it takes place, at the home of some clever people, certainly, who really knew how to take charge of things, don't you think, experts in cruelty, and who were chatting away loudly in front of an aviary, what makes me think that? and I don't really know if it was the animals' helplessness that moved me or the simple nearness of those dangerous insects, drawn into their trap).

6

This being Ted's way of bringing everyone's minds back into sync, he begins to play you a tune that also has the effect of bringing a sort of kindliness into his face, I'd even stick my neck out and call it a gentleness of sorts that's hard to explain but that wraps around his head and shoulders like a halo, too bad if that sounds a bit kitschy and sentimental, but the effect is undeniable, as though he is radiating a new, interior light born of a complex chemical process, some kind of electric friction between two worlds, because we understand that there exists, in all probability, in spheres inaccessible to us, and far far beyond this courtyard, a transcendent place where the music he's playing already exists, in an ideal form, a distant melody to which Ted is lending his sharp ear, and that he intends to hear clearly—not giving a damn for the considerable remoteness nor the ethereal nature of that separate universe—over the course of the many immaterial roundtrips he will take in order to reproduce it now in our presence, Ted the miraculous messenger, whose halo in its opaline luminosity gives such clear evidence of supernatural power that it, this halo, is all we see, and Mary, I don't have to tell you, is especially sensitive to it as, chin in the palm of her hand, she lets her gaze wander, sometimes scanning Ted's features, increasingly geometric due to his concentration, sometimes losing itself in the increasingly haloed countryside around him.

Our Ted, whose eyelids, with their delicate systems of irrigation, spreading a net of minuscule vessels over their surface, are lowered to his guitar, launches into the threnody.

What we have is the tale of a lonesome hero who roams the land, oh yeah.

Ted's voice is, how to describe it? a voice with a reach and tessitura that makes it baritone, as far as I can tell, a voice with a foot in each camp, medial, intermediate, more of a consensus-seeking voice, with frequent inflections that seem like concessions, somewhat submissive movements, perhaps, toward his listeners, but still generous, offhandedly tolerant, or anyhow, that's what we hear in it.

And, simultaneously, this voice—which, of course, calls upon the phonatory system for its different phases, well, I'll just give you an overall view, the musculo-membraneous folds of the vocal cords, the larynx containing them, glottis included as well, the uvula dangling there, lonely and fleshy, but vibrating as uvular consonants go by in their departure from the back of the tongue, which, generally speaking, acts like a supple sea lion, happily flopping forward to play tag with the teeth (you sometimes catch sight of it, pink, muscular, faintly dotted with delicate papillae, expertly applied), and while the lips, ah, Ted's lips, according to the shape they adopt, modulate the flow of sound coming out, the facial sinuses, I'll continue with my overview, act more or less as minuscule resonance chambers, and the breath too is called upon to contribute, the lungs, the stomach I think, the abdominal muscles, all of this is part of the corporeal process of singing, filling the cowboy's musculature and mucosal membranes with an energy that is very much physical, very much of the body, one that Mary finds quite moving, what else can you expect—this voice seems to distill, in its vibrations, in its own personal timbre, in its fluctuations, which seem involuntary, something like autobiographical fragments, hatched from its chance variations, letting their secret and untranslatable forms emerge (boo!), tenuous, encoded segments that then float into the air. With the result that, for example, hearing him, twisting a wisp of hair around your index finger, you have the feeling (I'm speaking for Mary, essentially) that you're on the verge of knowing the entire story of the person possessing that voice, a voice that conveys in its inflections a sporadic, incomprehensible tale, but one that is, nonetheless, being offered up, so delicately, to you alone.

This story that the voice brings with it is inscribed in the principal verbal filigree of the song, with its explicit plot, and all three listeners are drawn in, though each of them holds his or her body on their chairs in their own manner, a manner that very probably could give us some indication of how they each are picturing the elements of the song's story, bringing to bear, without giving it a thought, their own pile of memories, memories that show up and shape, in a subtle, subterranean manner, the work of representation in which they are now immersed, each of them creating his own little vision of the song's lonely hero, one that necessarily diverges to some degree from that of his neighbor, reprocessing, if you will, the few bits of information he receives on the basis of his own experience of the world, his particular way of doing things, with the vaguely egocentric but entirely excusable desire to attribute some of the features of one's own universe to the realms of fiction (occasionally feeling the delight of recognition whereby, look, you yourself are reflected in the tale, for a moment or two, knowing exactly what it's all about), I won't bother explaining the process in detail.

In their minds they follow the silhouette—three silhouettes, therefore, each listener painting one for themselves, with un-verifiable variations—of this hero whose vertebral column oscillates on his mount as the scenery goes by.

The cushioning between his vertebra gets a little roughed up, but otherwise he passes through the villages on his route without a scratch, handling his firearm with as much skill as reluctance (a Colt .41, the butt of which is nicely carved), always with the appearance of following some private thought that provides his gaze with a sort of double focus in which the abstract image of this thought is superimposed onto the foreground of each scene he is given to live through.

A thought that, if you like, because it intervenes like so in each situation confronting him, gives our rider a certain superiority, preventing him from getting lost in the moment, keeping him aloof from all the foolishness a pure and simple presence in the world can lead to when one is totally committed to what one is doing, with no going back.

Ted again takes up the refrain about the lonely hero, who roams across the land / oh yeah. Pistols at his side, nonstop / not a glance toward the crop / *oh yeah*. Hmm, looking for a way to make a song rhyme, one will often, as you've no doubt noticed, find oneself inclined to make slight thematic distortions that are more or less felicitous, and so there you are, going along with these sudden agricultural variations, led to imagine some field of corn when this hero's itinerary is far more likely to take him through a wild countryside, punctuated with nothing more than pebbles and rocks shaped like ruins, as a general rule, and perhaps, at the absolute pinnacle of local plant life, some cacti.

The fable that Ted's voice is conveying to his guests' ears is probably less rustic in its original, prose version than in this musical adaptation, even though, inside the phylactery of the thoughts of the hero in question, the vague outline of a cottage can be seen to peep through, a cottage with a fence around it, and on its doorstep a young woman whose features are indistinct, and who represents the utopia of a wife, *oh yeah*.

Mary has no difficulty projecting her own features onto this indistinct figure, at least to the extent that one is really able to know one's own features, am I right? since we only pay attention to our faces when we're contemplating ourselves with some anxiety, and rarely surprise them actually interacting with the world (supposing we've managed to cast a calm, completely disinterested eye at ourselves, this quick glance only allows us to have some idea of our faces in their inanimate phase, that is to say a thousand miles away from the mobility they certainly must demonstrate in conversation; and as to chance verifications of, say, Mary's face reflected in whatever surface—look, there I am!—usually these still leave one with a certain feeling of uncertainty when the furtive inspection is over). There's only one thing that's certain about one's own face, which is that you are completely ignorant of the expression it would wear if you stood that way on a doorstep with your eyes focused on the twist in the road burrowing into the nearby hills in the hope of soon seeing the silhouette of the one bringing you, how shall I put it? an emotional base, sexual pleasure, not to mention those brief, transcendent, piquant moments of sentimental intoxication that occasionally enliven one's life.

He roams the land, *oh yeah.*

Bit by bit, the attention of each listener now turns off down a different path, dividing the tale sung by Ted into episodes that have nothing to do with his story, some of these looking ahead as they begin to generate plans for the rest of the day, others bound to some near or distant past, and still others focused on the down-to-earth present moment. Dirk, for example, suddenly spots a rough patch on the table and gently feels out its smooth outline, seeking in this excrescence, this spot, this line meandering through the wood, some vaguely figurative equivalent, zoomorphic more than anything else, I think, while the pensive hero of the song continues his progress through the ochre countryside.

Oh yeah.

Leaving the aleatoric surface of the table, Dirk turns a loving gaze upon his hammock with the chiropterous silhouette that we've already noted, and where, if you return to the ranch an hour later, you'll find him, with the still-shriveled fabric of its wings spread out, hung up by its other end now on the gatepost of the corral, having thus acquired a rather potbellied aspect as a result of the occupant filling its paunch.

At best a bare or socked foot will emerge from this textile shell (I'm telling you this now because, in fact, we'll be somewhere else during Dirk's siesta), the presence of this sock in no way ruling out the persistent nudity of a big toe, so that the visitor approaching it will gradually see, more and more clearly, the vaguely tetragonal shape of the ingrown nail digging into the flesh that pops out in two lateral bulges, red and painful (as to the absent half-moon, it has vanished beneath the skin), on either end, while it will present, on the other side, the fleshy one, to the three chestnuts, who, having an idle moment, will be able to contemplate the sight, the undulating fields of its papillary ridges, at their leisure.

Sometimes an arm too will spill over the edge of the cloth, a testing arm that, in short, leaves base in order to measure the outside temperature, wondering about the degree of heat or, roughly, the densitometric level of the air, and in order to report back as to the immediate effects these elements might have, anticipating in the best of times the new ease with which one's body will be able to move around out there once it gets up, or else, more often, on the contrary, the degree of resistance likely to be opposed to it, in the name of opacity, by the air, thick with heat, circulating in a gaseous environment unfavorable for movement.

And he shot his way across the map . . .

It also happens sometimes, of course, that you get sidetracked thinking about what you're going to do next today, this subject suddenly starts nagging at you and, for a moment, keeps your mind from concentrating on the hoofbeats and the actions and movements of the song's hero managing his horse, whether your plans include some ambitious project or just a sort of abrupt return to the few practical obligations providing the rhythm of your existence, obligations that both bore you to tears and justify you as you carry them out.

And while the horseback rider in the threnody is repairing his mount's breast harness, it certainly had to be done, or its noseband, absolutely necessary, you think, in spite of yourself, of all the conditions you'll have to meet in order to accomplish whatever small thing you're planning to do in the way it's meant to be done.

He surely did . . .

Our thirty-year-old's coccyx nerve, painfully prompted by his chair, sends its regards to its host's brain, causing this specimen to wriggle around in an attempt to find a better position, making himself reestablish the support provided by the tender bone in some other area, one bordering it but not sticking out quite so far. These goings-on continue for a bit, each solution decided upon proving just as temporary as the last, given that each presents several new drawbacks of its own. If you've managed to put some plumper (and even then, not by much) part of your body between the too-hard seat of a chair and your skeletal structure, where it is meant to serve as a small, natural cushion, almost immediately, as everyone knows, you'll have trouble with the greatly narrowed surface of your base, to say nothing of how your vertebral column is now twisted, and the latter, weakened by your biography, which has not, let's face it, been all that comfortable, nights on the damp ground and days on horseback, won't be able to stand this treatment for long. So, as a result, you have to maneuver over into some different twist, compensatory but soon just as painful in turn and, no longer able to keep still on this stiff, not very accommodating chair, you let your eyes go from Dirk to Ted and back, systematically and mechanically scanning the two in a process that keeps you fairly absorbed, enumerating the ways they are dissimilar, as in the game of Spot the Difference.

. . . he shot his way across the map. Oh yeah.

The final plucked chord vibrates a bit and the wave hangs for a moment, alone in the air of the courtyard, the last one, with no other wave coming to erase it, spreading unimpeded to its natural extinction, a slow extinction that seems to start and stop, break off wherever a bit of atonic, silence-producing oxygen mixes into it, segments it, severs it, so that each now-autonomous segment finally ends up bursting and being reabsorbed.

III
the siesta

1

We all know the texture of a man's daydreams when he's gone back up to his hotel room during the most oppressive hours of the afternoon, forced by the heat to minimize his movements, indeed to reduce them to nothing save those required by breathing (his body sunk as deep as possible into the scanty substance of his mattress and then that's it), and, his intellect itself being completely exhausted, limp all over, demanding its share of rest, it heads a little off-camera to sit and doze, thereby allowing his thoughts to wander wherever they please, nice girls, a little silly, who don't show him anything particularly new, alas.

Such a man begins, I believe, by going back over his most recent actions (he left Dirk and Ted Lange's courtyard, having gotten up shortly after the end of the song sung by Ted, who had put his guitar down again and was in fact the first to take tacit leave of the group and walk off, zigzagging toward the corral, while thinking about what? Mary, for her part, had walked off in the direction of the laundry, and Dirk, his old friend, hadn't even waved to them, so occupied was he in the contemplation of his hammock, in which, given the time, he is bound to have lain his body now, which probably has it weighed down like some potbellied (as we already mentioned) fabric monster between the low wall and the gatepost to the corral), for those are the thoughts that serve to fill in this sort of transitional gap, the ones that set up a reassuring connection, if you will, between these two early episodes of the day, letting the preceding moment spill over slightly into the present moment (inside the room the fragile image of the ranch floats like a design painted on cellophane) in an invaluable intersection, a sustained representation of continuity that probably serves the purpose of reassuring our siesta-hopeful, helping him settle into a coherent space-time.

At first these recollections are simple, neat and tidy, incontestable.

The scene of the friends' successive goodbyes is contemplated in order of their departure. I'll expand a little: Ted goes first, heading off as if the ground were pitching beneath his feet, as if it were, let's suppose, the bridge of a ship, where he is a heaving, novice cabin boy, or else as if it were the flank of a sizeable animal expanding and then contracting as its breath comes and goes, an animal it would be better to allow to sleep, so please tread carefully; Dirk second, Dirk who had already left the group without moving from his chair, Dirk who had abandoned the empty envelope of his body, absent by way of an entirely inner absence, in which his thoughts, swarming around the cloth of his hammock, even pinching it in various places, had, through the sheer power of his mental faculties, successfully deployed it in his imagination, proffered it, concave and welcoming, all ready to receive him, with the result that a transparent version, a simulacrum of Dirk, had risen from this heavy, material body and gone off to stretch out and dream; then Mary, who had certainly noticed Dirk's abdication, and, probably worrying she was about to be abandoned, preferred to quit the table before our thirty-year-old, like any small and very busy young woman who has already given you enough of her time.

Then thought goes digging around in the things that slightly preceded these goodbyes and sprinkles our thirty-year-old's imaginings with a few particularly visual moments (there's the Siamese shadow of Dirk and Ted against the rough plaster of the low wall, for instance, the projection of the contours of their bodies, which, though disconnected in actual fact, had at that instant come to be stuck together in a fleeting partnership) that it further enlivens with, in all honesty, the memory of Mary's arrival. Look at how, as the young woman walks, the tips of the bright blue satin ribbon holding her wide-brimmed bonnet delicately flutter and flap at breast level. The detail is quite precise, but you can start to manipulate this memory by continually updating it, repeating it indefinitely, just as often as you wish, at varying speeds, making these photograms linger as they roll past, slow-motion shots in which the satin whips languorously, lavishly against the heavy cotton of her dress, or sometimes more quickly, the effect rapid and comic and avenging the dreamer in his desire.

It all begins to get a little spicier when these same memories are subjected to new bends and twists, for the sake of introducing some, why not, romantic ingredients into his day, all the more romantic when you can develop your theme however you like, modifying reality as it actually took place—just a bit—so that one plays a more important part in the story.

For example, our thirty-year-old now has a try at constructing a few perfectly fictional dialogues between Mary and himself, on either side of the table located in the courtyard, or, better, imagines other departures, superior to the real one, with him accompanying Mary back to the cleaners, I assume, rather than letting her leave all by herself, thus creating a bubble of time they share, that's a sweet prospect. They walk side by side, who knows how long, down the main street, clambering along the porches, brushing against walls when there's no covered terrace and barely four inches of roof, perhaps, overhanging the vertical surface of the façade to edge the ground below with a darker ribbon, sometimes bumping into each other in their haste to plunge into the patches of shade each time they see one. They make as great an effort as possible to stay intact in the shadow, occasionally letting an elbow, an arm spill over and get hit by a great splash of light. And yes, when, in spite of themselves, they must venture out into a sunny area, they happily trample their own neatly condensed silhouettes beneath the soles of their shoes.

Ten times, a hundred times, he goes back over their sudden swerves, the way they would dive under the roofs, their jostling hopscotch among the shadows—shadows, the freewheeling mind of our thirty-year-old rhapsodizes, that we carry with us almost everywhere we go, reshaped in daylight anamorphoses and erased when overcast skies finally rid us of these monkey-selves busily imitating us in their obstinate and grotesque foreshortenings.

Once these countries of very recent memory have been sufficiently explored, and since we've already, necessarily, adorned them with some imagined variations that we find more than a little tempting, our thirty-year-old's daydreams soon head off into the just-slightly-more-distant past to seek out certain events that took place some ambiguous length of time ago in this very town, and among these events, a tiny, particular one eating away at him, a stupid incident that absolutely does not deserve being remembered, an annoyance you should have been able to smother but that sticks its nose back up, here, just when you were hoping to spend two peaceful hours letting your mind wander over the harmless memories that elbow their way up into the light, Hey! Remember me? says the annoyance you would have liked to forget, and yes, up it comes, exposing itself from every angle on the stage of your thought. How bizarre, this tendency to cling to this memory, you say to yourself, while it swaggers around, how strange, adding to the annoyance you've already experienced the irritation of knowing you'll let yourself be submerged in remembering it all over again.

This tiny, defiant memory, which distinguishes itself so clearly from the heap of fragile, scarcely sustained subjects briefly popping up in our man's mind only to disintegrate immediately (those particular subjects would be just as hard for me to catch, in order to show you, as chasing butterflies with a net held out in front of me—picture it—while tripping over lumps of earth pushed up by moles: likely to lose my unpredictable Lepidoptera if I start paying attention to the ground I'm walking over, but unable to catch anything so long as I'm falling all over the place), this thought, more vigorous than the others, no longer forming a single long wave along with them, driving its roller onto the beach, this thought, a sturdy residue rather than foam, though still, well, how should I put it, not a thought of the first order, just one that happens to carry inside it the memory of one of those little, unsettled hostilities that can always reemerge, you know, a false note resounding unpleasantly in your ear, a situation you hadn't been able to wriggle out of and that comes back to haunt you with its ridiculous specter, right at nap time, this thought, yes, relates to an incident that occurred at Harry's, you saw him this morning, remember, the acromegalic silhouette barely visible way back in the darkness of his shop.

The lighting of the scene itself demonstrates a kind of conflict, with the almost livid glow of a candle on one side of the tableau jousting with, on the other, the more refluent corpuscles of "available light," as they say, flowing through the filter of a dirty window into the deep darkness of the room.

In this agonistic atmosphere, the whitish photonic splashes deriving from the outside world, and the others—waxy yellow—emitted by the wick that burns while serving to make the scene seem even darker around its periphery, splatter onto Harry's face where they repeatedly dispute the ownership of a few square inches, if that, of skin, and begin to engage with the peaks and valleys of its bony volume, making its protrusions even more salient.

The sound of the little bell set ringing by a device attached to the door of the General Store makes Harry materialize instantly when it opens, as if his body with its undefined extremities were being born out of the sound itself, despite the tenuous nature of this crystalline ring by comparison with the substantial, wholly dissimilar silhouette emanating from it like some disproportionate and improbable consequence.

The scene takes place during the period when our thirty-year-old, having just arrived, was new to the village; Harry sizes up the stranger (whom he later, moreover, will persist in calling "Stranger" on the few occasions he has cause to speak to him, as if it were a proper name) with a gaze that is, you might say, completely uncharitable. The Stranger consents to this examination without lowering his eyes, spending these moments of scrutiny by unhooking his gun belt and placing it on the counter, with the tacit purpose of having its value appraised as part of a trade-in he hopes he can use, might as well just explain all the details, wanting to figure how much more he'd need to and/or would be prepared to pay in order to get that other, newer looking gun belt that he's already spotted through the shop window.

Without taking his eyes from our thirty-year-old's face, Harry begins his inspection of the aforementioned gun belt by means of a meticulous palpation, one that isn't exactly hurried.

While we await his verdict, let's take a quick look at the heteroclite objects piled up everywhere in his store, often not sorted particularly well, so you can find, let's see, reins tangled up around a checked blanket which is, itself, flopped over some doilies whose lacy edges, like the hoofed feet of some undetermined species, are trying to get out from under the wooly mass crushing down on them; heavy blue cotton pants folded in with some flags; boots, sometimes mismatched, relegated to a wooden box with some leather valises—a few so carefully shut that it by no means goes without saying that anyone will ever be able to open them again, because when they go unused the stinking things are quick to seize up, so that customers can persist for a long while skinning their fingertips on a reluctant latch, until finally their upper bodies jerk backwards in a startled arc when the thing abruptly deigns to open just when they least expect it, provoking, when it gives in like this, with no warning whatsoever, an exaggerated aftershock that's never quite curbed in time; though other valises, on the contrary, gape wide open, permitting the immediate examination of their entrails, but also making it quite clear that getting them closed again is probably out of the question (because of this, Harry will give you a special deal if you want, though it might not be much of a discount, since, after all, you just have to wrap your new valise with a cinch or a belt or string, depending on what you have available, and then it'll work as well as any other receptacle you'd use to carry your things in, if that's all you want)—while in another box there are more blankets, some of them fringed and others edged with satin binding, a small cloth barrier that holds back edges that would otherwise tend to run off in wild unravellings—all of these on sale as well but, at the same time, serving to protect from the ever-likely possibility of breakage the sensitive bellies of pottery pitchers, adorned more often than not with tattoos of sometimes geometric and sometimes floral designs, I don't know which you prefer, along with two or three badly stacked saucers whose circumferences aren't devoid of cracks showing their dull earthen flesh, the unvarnished skin revealed by the wound of a missing shard.

As far as china is concerned, the stock is essentially composed of hand-painted faience and glazed earthenware pottery imported from France (specifically La Rochelle for the former and Saint-Ouen for the latter). It's rather rare that you find a Chinese gentleman on one of these pieces—with a pipe, chasing dragonflies. Most often there's a central rose accompanied by another in bud or some animal figure produced by the same workshop that Henri Brevet, who directed it in the seventeen hundreds and a little into the eighteen, finally turned over to his mother-in-law, whose name, I'll just mention in passing, was Marguerite Boucher.

This particular plate, however, stands out from all the rest. Just look at that cabin with a fence, the bifid tree separated into two bouquets of foliage, and, I'm not making this up, a man seen from behind, wearing a hat, seated on a riverbank and fishing while six starlings fly above him in the bleached-out sky.

There is also a miniature ewer somewhere on these shelves, as well as a candlestick in old silver, you can take your time just looking around, here's a plain and simple pot, a somewhat more ornate vase, look and see if there's anything you like, this oil lamp, a little grimy, but once it's cleaned up, or wait, this pewter platter, a bit rustic, that would be a nice souvenir, or something in copper, this rosewood octant with its ivory and polished brass, this surveyor's bidirectional compass, this portable sundial with an axial line, not too badly damaged, or this box of measuring tools for making maps and signed Meunier et Gourdin. All right, what if you bought a knickknack at Harry's and took it home with you, you could put it on your mantelpiece (a coffee table would work too, that low table you have) and every time you went to sit on your sofa it would be right there where you could see it, reminding you of our thirty-year-old's adventures. It would complement you, to some extent, and when your friends come to visit and notice it, a knickknack that wasn't there last time, if I'm not mistaken, maybe even picking it up to turn it around in the horizontal light entering through your window, or coming vertically from your ceiling light (a simple attachment, or, okay, just a bulb hanging from a wire, it doesn't make any difference), they might ask, politely, just for the sake of knowing, and as much out of their interest in you as out of curiosity about the object in question, And this, where does it come from, where did you find it, where did you buy it, and you would reply Ah, that, it comes from *Western*, and, putting the object back where they found it, they would reply Oh, okay (probably they've never heard of it), and you could explain, making them sit across from you in an overstuffed armchair (they're your friends, an old cushion is just fine), and start to tell them about the adventures of our thirty-year-old. You would light a cigarette for them with your lighter, which is decorated with a picture of wherever it was you went for your last vacation, before putting its flame to your own with a significantly resolute gesture (or, as an alternative, you could pass around some chewing-gum, butter cookies, ginger snaps, mocha macaroons; you could serve them apple brandy, or whatever suits them), and you would begin, It's the story, etc., and your guests (drawing on their cigarettes, or chewing their bubble gum, making beautiful bubbles from time to time that burst in time to serve as emphatic punctuation for certain moments in your tale, or crumbling their cookies, biting into a macaroon after having unstuck the top half so as to admire the cream that's now getting a bit hard in the middle and giving off a different smell, or sipping their Calvados brought back from Trouville) wouldn't find your narrative hospitality at all displeasing, just try it and see.

You're also free to find this pitcher slightly too touristy, this oil lamp somewhat artificial, but wait, that old painting that we hadn't yet noticed, a little dark because of its varnish, a rather unusual still life if you think about it, wherein, next to each other, either because it's what the painter happened to have at hand or because he assembled it on purpose, like a rebus, there are three round loaves of bread, two of them intact and the third broken to let the whiteness of its crumb show, an earthenware fruit-bowl speckled with a blue design and from which emerge the aerodynamic shapes of some extremely pointed figs, their skin sparkling with white highlights, an evenly woven wicker basket holding pale peaches with deep, shadowy grooves, one of which, escaped somehow, has come to rest on the surface of the table, at the bottom of the tight, pyramidal group of the others, where it is delivering, perhaps, a random monologue—sometimes a poor little excluded thing hoping to return to its brethren, envying their placid sociability, and sometimes an entity free at last now and preparing to take off on its own, though, at heart, still hesitant—and in the foreground, slightly off to the right, a pewter dish where, curiously, three open oysters sit enthroned, their yellow-gray flesh (still quivering?) stands out against the pearly background of their shells. You wonder, as you lift the painting up to eye-level, your two arms more or less outstretched, yes? or else more or less retracted, depending on your particular type of optical pathology, well, you wonder what sea these bivalve lamellibranch mollusks are meant to have come from, a sea licking against what land, edging what geographies, a sea whose stubborn tidal movements, rosy sunrises, and grandiose sunsets you would like to picture, mentally, along with all those marine props that make seacoast towns so pretty, what sea, I ask you.

This painting isn't disproportionately large and, over your mantel, it would give your place quite a nineteenth-century look, not bad at all, which might begin to work in an interesting way against the other, more obviously modern, pieces of furniture, I'm just giving you my honest opinion.

Still, if you prefer something smaller, here's an engraving, that, should the occasion arise, could be put away in a drawer, if, for instance, you're in the mood to change the décor some day, a picture of, I'd say, a dance scene, sketched in the moonlight, with someone playing the mandolin at the foot of a couple, with a nice landscape in the background, it's pretty too, really, it's up to you.

About the three oysters and the seas from which they came, the people who landed on those formerly unknown beaches suddenly come to mind, new people, inexperienced, having left their parents behind on the old continent where, weighed down with sadness, they had been seen as complete losses, not much use anymore. Stricken with a vague, futile affection, you imagine the withered faces of these parents whimpering at the dock, dirty old handkerchiefs balled up in the palms of their hands now that they've stopped waving them like white seagulls along with all the other people around them who look like they're standing in the middle of a cotton aviary, still undulating their avian fabrics at the ends of their arms and presenting the perfect picture of a thousand crazed and impotent birds, vainly beating their wings in a ballet whose choreography delivers their message of good will, yes, these people, the ones left behind, are still brave enough to wish those who are departing from them well. And, on the contrary, as the boat cleaves its way further into the waves, those departing feel themselves relieved of their emotions, left behind along with the land, squinting their eyes toward a still-empty horizon (well, empty of everything except sea and sky: one on top of the other in a simple geometry), imagining all sorts of fantastic things to which, they think, the wind is taking them.

While you are attending to your purchases or merely snooping around, Harry is fingering the rough spots on the papilliferous leather of the gun belt as if he were reading its history in braille.

And, well, what a turbulent story it is, with tough nights, muddy beds on damp humus, storms, rains with no shelter, snow, look, the leather is burned over there, dangerous trajectories through clawing branches, stories of narrow and protracted escapes, not to mention the implacable sun, the withering dryness; the belt inventories the times it was scored by grains of sand, scratched by cactus thorns, along with an interlude on a train, because there are slightly greasy deposits of carbon dioxide on it that must have come from the locomotive's smokestack; and finally there's some fighting chronicled there too, the fingerprints of angry men, traces of body-to-body combat, that's more or less a complete list.

Throughout this entire digital reading our thirty-year-old's heart was in his boots because he hadn't expected any such biographical disclosures.

On the subject of his own life, you've probably noticed that he's the type who tends to clam up, if that expression makes any sense in such a non-aquatic milieu; *mute as a mule* works a whole lot better here.

As soon as our thirty-year-old's epic has been read in its entirety, the brutal deciphering barely having ceased, Harry pushes the gun belt back across the counter without even considering it necessary to provide any sort of explanatory exposition for his rejection.

How do you think our thirty-year-old reacted then, seeing—one—his hope for acquiring a new gun belt dashed, then—two—receiving the double insult of a rejection and what's more one unjustified by any polite statement (the sequencing here is summary but random, and shouldn't be taken as implying a hierarchy of any kind), and, finally—three—finding himself partially denuded in this way?

One of those sonsabitches (my spell-check speaks up at this point, but complains that it has "no spelling suggestions") from Liberty Valance's gang would, of course, have put his gun belt right back on, calmly, taking time to tie the strip holding the holster to his thigh, and only then would have pulled out his pistol and fired, once, twice at Harry, withdrawing as the shopkeeper's body collapses with a crash, with or without a reverse shot at the wild-eyed gaze of the dying man slumping down behind his counter. But a hero like ours, on a slightly tighter rein, is able to swallow his humiliation: certain, inside, of later demonstrating—and on precisely the terms he desires—his true value, and that's why our thirty-year-old, going back out of the General Store without a word, made his way back to his hotel, carrying something bitter, as they say, in his heart—a bitterness that pierces through him anew whenever he thinks of this scene.

2

Tossing around a few harmless ideas, as well as certain others, which, hurtful but nonetheless carrying little weight, come to prick him with their stubborn stimuli (so that his siesta time is a variegated affair in which pleasure and annoyance listlessly dispute the territory of his vacant mind), our thirty-year-old's attention sometimes comes back to the décor of the room he's returned to, a room about which he himself has chosen nothing whatsoever, neither its shape nor its furnishings, having arrived there one already bygone day and then just never having left again, exhausted I think by his travels and deciding to wait there for what couldn't help but happen in any event, he told himself, each day bringing him mathematically closer to its advent, and each morning, always begun on the porch in the precarious and bumpy rocking of an old chair, in the manner we've so recently observed, presenting its prospect to him on the horizon.

What immediately strikes the eye of whomever (that's us, I think) enters this room for the first time is the obvious distinctiveness between the set, neat and tidy, and the person of our thirty-year-old, still wearing boots, legs crossed on a bedspread whose openwork stitches let the ivory cotton of the sheet show through, wearing all his clothes except for his gun belt, dangling at the moment on the back of the single armchair (so modest in dimension that it's hard, really, to see how the body of a grown man could fit into it, and most especially, of course, that of our tall and vigorous protagonist), the same old worn gun belt that he hadn't been able to swap and whose chewed up, blistered leather contrasts starkly with the delicate pastel fabric cover on which it lays, while his revolver, a Smith and Wesson—that it's perhaps time for me to warn sensitive souls is extremely likely to be used by our thirty-year-old before the end of this book—is lying on the gray-white marble surface of a walnut night table (with its little drawer in pretty good, usable shape; it would work really well at your place, or mine, but I worry it's probably not for sale).

What's at stake is this imbalance between the somewhat, let's say, rough, right-out-of-the-box nature of the individual in question and the vaguely floral décor of his surroundings.

Take, for example, this oil lamp, placed on the table, covered with a damask cloth, where our thirty-year-old has made a habit of cleaning the barrel of his Smith and Wesson. You'd probably have expected a reservoir of tinted glass in ochre or brown, but no, not at all, it's a porcelain lamp-belly with a white background on which forget-me-nots and buttercups clearly cross stems.

Its nice little country appearance echoes the design of the washbasin where likewise the faience is adorned with several *Rosae multifoliae* whose fuchsia, straw-yellow, and bright orange petals form cheerful patches.

And I'm not even going to mention the embroidered alphabet hanging on the wall in its gilded frame.

But the highlight of the room is the dressing screen, whose moving, articulated panels, let me point out, are obviously intended to be stood between the basin and the window like a partition (or between the basin and the inside of the room, if there happens to be a visitor) when our man partially strips over that small aquatic parallelogram to do some washing up (stripping entirely only occurs on the ground floor in the bathtub provided for that purpose; but don't expect to see our hero's body, moderately concealed by the dirty water, slightly opaque because of the saponiferous substances disintegrating in it and not really obscuring the sculptural detail of a torso, the crumpled and touching little protuberance of a nipple, or the amply displayed water lily of his genitals—today isn't bath day).

Said panels are covered with stretched cloth wherein a pastoral and romantic work force are frolicking and a quick panoramic shot allows you to pick out the few recurrent figures: a shepherdess carrying her pitcher to the spring (skirt skillfully pleated, free hand lodged in the curve of her waist where it looks like an island close to the continent whose coastal outline it follows, all the while threatening further secession; her foot is already stepping on the polished coping of the well where a spreading ivy creeps); a group of shepherds conversing under a plane tree (one of them, more voluble than the others, punctuates his speech with a graceful wave of the arm while the other three are content to listen, inserting I think a few daydreams of their own devising into their silence); a lone, stylish shepherd driving two very wooly sheep ahead of him (he has a noble look, this one, and is whistling, I think); a shepherd and shepherdess sitting together off to the side on the trunk of a fallen tree serving them as an improvised bench (a godsend that it would have been a sin to pass up, offering a natural seat for their encounter as well as a chance, don't you think, to try out their rhetoric, which will hopefully lead to more, if it turns out they're compatible); and finally this mule-driver, who, more introverted than the others, is seated on his mount and goes by at an unhurried pace, passing in front of a grove of trees in the background.

When you see the face of our thirty-year-old in profile like this against the oh-so-neat and tidy bucolic scene, the first simile that comes to mind is that it's like a collage, since it all looks as though this same face, originally figuring in a real and rustic landscape against the knotty trunks of a place called Sevenoaks, had been cut out of that first image, which seemed to be his natural setting, only to be placed over this new background, which has no relation to it, and where it clashes, because, being so foreign to the décor of this piece of toile de Jouy, it seems to have been forcibly, as I said, transferred here via the authoritarian action of a pair of scissors.

But, if I may venture an opinion, your simile is not entirely correct. It's an undeniably interesting comparison in that it makes a new, original image shine in the background of the scene we're actually looking at, that is, the image from which our thirty-year-old's face is meant to have come, a lost image, now ravaged, where the two crossed blades of your alleged scissors have left, where there should be a face, nothing but a hole with a little channel leading to it from the edge of the photograph, as if to a lake—alas, an image that, if it had not been mutilated, would have shown you this man who dwelt there, in a sort of constant and indisputable contact with this solid vegetation, accustomed to the great outdoors and posing in front of fields bordered by the massive shapes of oak trees, in front of orchards, in an absolute continuity, by means of which the nature surrounding him, modified by himself time and time again, following traditional methods of cutting, seeding, and other tasks, would seem to have transformed him in return, having gone from being a material and ordinary landscape to become an inner landscape as well.

However, where your comparison errs is that, in a collage, the transferred face, necessarily ignorant of having been moved, preserves the same expression it wore originally—a rather happy look, an extension of its former conformity—even if the new surroundings in which it appears differ from its proper location in every way. It's probably this discrepancy precisely—not just between its physical self and this new, alien locale into which it's been plunged, but also between the state of its soul, expressing its old continuity, its transfixed contentment, arising from its previous situation, and the obviously incompatible characteristics displayed by the new background into which it's now been pasted—that makes it so much fun for people to contemplate such a collage, that make them burst out laughing when they see the man, so out of place and yet so satisfied, trapped within surroundings that don't suit him at all, about which he knows nothing, and from which, if he were capable of coming to life to think it over, he would be pretty eager to escape.

However, in the situation under discussion, this very discrepancy is, on the contrary, sensed by the face: it has become a constant conflict, it is pervasive.

See how our man's contours, rather than fitting exactly into the room, seem to have contrived something like a blurry coating to separate his body from the bedroom's space, like a hazy shell, a husk, yes, like a husk of hazy air that follows his morphology from head to toe and keeps it from coming in contact with things. A sheath, formed from the extremely turbulent circulation of particles of indecision, faced with this very incompatibility and the confusion that arises from acknowledging the fact. What radiates from our man is his discomfort concerning the aforementioned incongruity, and his worrying about how to lessen it. Are we going to be able to accomplish such a task, the aforementioned particles ask themselves as they race back and forth madly—or even know how to start, which is the question asked most often, filtering from their ichthyoidal and disconcerted lips. A flexible partition of air, hugging his shape—like a wetsuit, if you will—seems to flow all around him as if something like a basic ontological difference existed in him that would make the direct immersion of this body in this room simply impossible, its friction in this atmosphere untenable, each action only capable of execution if the limb in motion is wrapped in a watertight sheath separating it from the irreconcilable universe of the room in which it is, nonetheless, being carried out.

This strangeness, however, is occasionally interrupted by certain happy moments when it almost disappears. With repeated frequentation, décor slowly changes, evolves to look more like you, because as we weave, at least, an optical connection with its elements from siesta to siesta, and one thing leading to another, you know how it goes, we become attached to our surroundings as though they were small metonymies of ourselves, we think that yes, somehow, they are extensions of our being, so that we no longer want to have them taken away, and each time our eyes return to them, it causes a sweet shock of recognition.

Inevitably, you yourself experience the way in which a place you frequently do some thinking, a permanent-feeling place like this room, or maybe just someplace that you happen to pace up and down, a square, or let's think bigger—a park, or the façades of houses you go by every day and that you've brushed past with your eyes so many times as you walk along talking to yourself that they've retained a few granules of your thoughts on their surfaces, the residue of sentences that you had formulated when you glanced at them, and that sometimes were actually comments about them, but more often were autonomous reflections on subjects that were, okay, either general (imagine some frantic summarizing of your own life, or maybe even a few thoughts about how things are going in the world at large, on the days you don't pull any punches) or else on a more modest scale, a specific event you were ruminating over like an old wad of pretty tasteless chewing gum that you nonetheless keep on chewing (indeed, some practical detail that you really have to take care of, a problem with how you use your time, leading you to juggle plans made in advance in order to slip this new task in where it might fit best, and it isn't necessarily that your days are particularly full, but just that, in this general inertia which after all is the way of life that suits you best, you are looking for ways to accommodate such responsibilities in ways

that will introduce the least disturbance, trying, if by chance another obligation emerges, to kill two birds with one stone, to
group things, to make fewer trips), after all you have plenty to
work with there and what goes on inside you doesn't ever run
out of gas when confronted by any one of these possible subjects; this experience that, I was saying, in addition to the places
where one spends one's time in soliloquies, and that might very
well not have any relation to you in the beginning, being disconnected, at first, to your history, or to those of any of your
relatives, and being moreover configured in a manner that you
probably wouldn't have chosen yourself, if anyone had asked
your opinion or for a little help with the decoration, some ar-
chitectural advice, and even those geraniums, look, that they've
put in the windows and that you go by several times a week
in this foreign city you've lived in for a while, their red-faced
patches, the vaguely thick-lipped shape of their petals, no, had
you been the people renting that place you wouldn't have put
geraniums out, but what, something more wild, blooming more
discreetly, mostly stalks, that would have also sported the peti-
oles of some fragile, crumply leaves, if, really, you were to hang
some sort of plant there, which, anyway, is yet another subject
you could chew away on; the experience, in short, of places like
that where it's a given that they aren't really in complicity with
you (whereas, don't you agree, in front of other places, though
setting foot there for the first time, you've said to yourself, once
in a while, that yes, this place is totally me, exactly the sort of
place where you could see yourself, with a sort of unexplainable,
intuitive recognition, probably due to some layers of your history that, by and large, you have forgotten, and would have been

unable to identify, except possibly with a good deal of effort—a not-necessarily-desirable result, because what good would it do you to have a better idea which memory no longer present in your consciousness happened to draw you to some particular color, some particular arrangement of things, since then you would be compelled, perhaps, to associate this sense of a simple, renewed continuity with life with the painful acknowledgement that that world, along with all its imperfections, no that's not the point, but all the embarrassments and sorrows it contains, and all the annoyances, is already gone, lost, so that this idea of loss, when you aren't really in a position to say good riddance to what's gone, given that all these moments, good and bad, are interwoven, and the crumbling away of time is, by nature, dreadful, this idea would have wrecked everything, substituting a futile nostalgia for your unexplained contentment), the experience of such places, I'm getting to it, by dint of wearing them down almost daily with your voluptuous inspections, corroding them as it were, scoring them with the invisible marks of the erosion you impress upon them by the repeated waves of the aforementioned voluptuous inspection, this deep searching, or it could well be because, as I said, you added a thick layer of your thoughts to them and, gradually, bit by bit, day after day, though this hadn't been their intent, being so dissimilar, these thoughts covered them with a filter just as impalpable but with a texture such that after a while it almost disguised their initial strangeness, cloaking them in the tawdry rags of your own daydreams; that such places, consequently, though so different from yourself at first glance, begin to reflect you, their existence in a certain sense domesticated by your thought, no longer living their own resistant, obscure, opaque lives as décor, speaking their untranslatable or discordant pieces, but quivering now at your approach, coming slyly out to meet you, like what? like the animal that you have living with you, perhaps, that you feed, take for walks, even talk to, actually pretty silly, with the result that it seems to understand you (and I wouldn't even be surprised if you went so far as to tell it a few secrets that you wouldn't tell your friends, and the canine being, recognizing perhaps four or five words of your vocabulary, the ones most frequently repeated, the most useful, had seemed to listen carefully, giving his approval to your every least confessional nuance), onto which you have projected something of yourself, creating—deep inside these façades, these trees or interior walls—your true diaries, the pages of the journal you will never really write, and that offer themselves up, fossilized there, for rereading each time you go by.

Well, that's exactly what happens to our thirty-year-old, who at the moment has a dual relationship with this room, which in its external particulars continues to clash physically with him and which nonetheless, in the way he presently looks at it, seems familiar to him, with a familiarity, how shall I put it, that, though not constant (he is still horrified sometimes, in brief moments of renewed objectivity on the subject, by the flowery porcelain belly of that oil lamp), is rather profound when functioning, so that he can let himself delve far enough into the design of this screen as to identify, briefly, and not of course with the fine-talking shepherd conversing with his fair lady, nor even with the most-introverted of the group of talkative men, but with the lonely muleteer who rides on the back of his hybrid animal born of ass and mare, and traverses the landscapes with an absentminded look upon his face.

Receptacle of the thoughts that he's distilled in it during his siestas, this room, by dint of accommodating them, welcoming them into its hidden recesses, letting them be grafted here and there, in a corner, onto the side of a piece of furniture, in the detail of a design, has ended up covered by another invisible, but ever-present, coating.

Without having in any way changed the layout of the room, without having removed any of its furniture, nor, I believe, added any, except for some temporary and minimal knickknack such as the presently collapsed body of his leather hat on the straw seat of the chair, looking there like a pet having a little time to itself, patiently dozing and waiting to see what might happen next, and which has the effect, in the décor, yes, of something like a signature, of a significant but nonetheless ad hoc reappropriation, in short, without having changed anything in the material circumstances of this room, he has, however, transformed it intangibly merely through his repeated internal monologues, the emotions he's felt there and which have filled the volume of the room with their fragile emanations before sticking on the walls, becoming incorporated, taking shelter in the hollows of whatever objects would let them in, in the thick layers of varnish, in a shape, a color, a line, so that now, when you look at them, they breathe that memory back out, whichever thought you'd been thinking, breathe it out again subtly, delicately, and secretly.

Of course, only someone who's felt these same emotions in this room can recognize what it's saying in return, how it turns those signals into a faint but insistent reminder, this achromatic layer woven there by your daydreams. It has the same sort of bond with its tenant that connects you to a confidant, in a sort of reciprocal subjection, in a sweet and fragile dependency.

That's why this room, which had seemed so dissimilar from its occupant when we came in, so foreign, has gradually let itself be made to resemble the person dwelling inside it, without his having to negotiate even the least rearrangement, without anyone having to make a request of the innkeeper, no, just through force of habit and projected daydreams, and has done this so well that, lined as it is with all the trains of thought that have been spun here, now, despite the strangeness of the choices of furnishings or color, it makes you feel pretty much right at home.

It is, thus, in this alternation between a renewed feeling of disparity between himself and his surroundings and this feeling of amazing closeness, the intimacy acquired with time, through layer after layer of the siestas spent there, and, in the end, creating this improbable, unverifiable, underlying resemblance, superimposed upon the sensation of strangeness more than replacing it, that our thirty-year-old returns in fits and starts to the scene at Harry's.

He mulls it over, adds the finishing touches, digs in a little further, the way you would tear the sore skin off at the edge of your nail, giving in to the urge to pester the reddish wound revealed by the epidermis as it's pushed farther and farther back, enlarging it, rather than letting it just hang there like that.

Every now and then our thirty-year-old applies another enticing denouement to his little wound, like a soothing ointment, rolls over on the bedspread into the fetal position best suited for this regressive rewriting of things, where finally events might turn out to his advantage, where, after all, the whole point is to make himself look a little better, making up for the harshness of concrete reality by means of fantasies that are, of course, evanescent and imaginary, but reinvigorating just the same.

Of these two or three more lighthearted versions of the affair, let's highlight the one in which Harry, having just read the gun-belt epic with his fingers, and more than happy at the prospect of coming into possession of such a proud hero's gun belt, gives our man, right then and there, exactly what he's asking for it, and even tosses in a few gifts from among the objects you'd taken stock of while poking around earlier, that almost-new pair of boots, for instance, which Harry only recently acquired (our man checks the uppers, both marked with the same embroidery, then holds them sole to sole to make sure they're the same size, perfect), that blanket, always useful in the mountains whenever our thirty-year-old decides to leave town (but there's no hurry, Harry wants to make this clear, yes, take your time, his face friendly, not at all concerned with making a sale), and then look, if he likes it, let's toss in that engraving you didn't notice just now, a night scene, two cowboys by a fire telling a few stories whose contents our man can well imagine in idle moments, in his room at the inn, having set the piece on his dresser, quietly contemplating it from his bed, hands crossed on his stomach and mind at peace.

Or does Harry intend to offer our man that still life, and does your imagination paint its terrible departure scene for you once again, and you tell yourself that, probably, it was the energy prevailing at the port as the frigates, warships, lighters, and so forth, I'm skipping some, were casting off, that must have given the people departing their homes forever confidence at the moment they boarded ship. Yes, the way everybody around them was bustling about, the sort of professionalism with which the men rolled barrels on the paving stones or tied rope around trunks, must have seemed a good omen. Only the effort, the skill, the haranguing, the stubborn and competent air of those employed on the docks could explain how the passengers were able to leave everything behind, giving the extraordinary nature of their departure a familiar appearance that had enabled them to set foot on the boats and stay there until they left their moorings.

Did they look back to shore as the cast-off rags of their past life grew distant; or, instead, did they stand on the bow like extra figureheads, chests thrust out, bodies firmer now because of the sense of moving ahead? And when, later, sails swelling, convex as waves, they must have had to confront storms, what did they think of then, tossed around beneath darkened skies, given that the distant horizons had now been replaced by nearby foam, threatening swells, making the sky and then the sea tip over, optically capsizing? Could they still hear their thoughts in the tumult of the waves crashing against the hull?

In another of these versions, Harry, having learned our man's story by indiscreet exploration of the gun belt with his fingers,

invites him to sit down in the back of the store, *Take that chair,*
he points, contenting himself with an old trunk, dark, studded
with hobnails, well, it doesn't matter much, and serves him a
glass of old whiskey that he made himself, something he keeps
for important occasions, corn liquor, really pretty good. Harry
in turn confides the story of his life through the sucking noises
that whiskey-drinking entails, confession being a very practical thing for a person taking a siesta in the heat of this long,
drawn-out afternoon to imagine, because if you're in top form
you can spend a lot of time thinking up all the details, which,
however, I'll spare you, because, though maybe it doesn't seem
like it, we're going to have more urgent business to deal with
soon. At the end of his tale, squaring things between himself
and our thirty-year-old, Harry's tactile indiscretion having
somehow been counterbalanced by his subsequent confidence,
the shopkeeper, willing to take our man's old gun belt, gives
him the one he lusted after in return, a beautiful, brand-new
gun belt, punctuating the exchange with a friendly pat on the
back to indicate that he is ignoring the difference in marketabil-
ity of the two properties, although objectively it's obvious that
he came out rather badly in this trade, which means that their
new friendship has created, if you will, an added value, and that
the financial loss has been recouped by emotional benefit he's
gained from the transaction.

Several other versions are still bouncing around in our thirty-
year-old's mind until, from one modest rebound to the next, the
bounces become more and more widely spaced, more and more
minuscule, and the chapter about Harry finally closes.

3

No guaranteeing, right, that this actual, minor, but upsetting scene at the General Store won't come back to torment him yet again, here or there, more fleetingly, less developed, just shooting its one little arrow and then taking off again, mocking, elusive, mischievous, you know what it's like, because no doubt you've felt yourself to be on the receiving end, at one time or another, in setbacks just like this one—feel free to slip in an example of your own, here—of one of these kinds of minor injustices, whereas, really, you were completely in the right; a scene that didn't change the course of your life in any way, but it's the idea of the injustice, isn't it, and how bizarre, after all, that whenever you're languidly letting your thoughts run on their own power, with the idea of granting yourself a pleasant moment of rest, you're still likely to see this tiny and yet aggravating episode, which reappears without any particular justification, rise out of the depths; what an odd thing that this anecdote, so unsubstantial and yet unpleasant, can still, alas, be summoned up, in spite of yourself, so to speak, and just because you had, with some confidence, given your mind permission to take itself wherever it wanted, allowing it, with the largesse of someone walking their favorite quadruped on an extendable leash, to pull the black line of its tether as far as it can go, watching it wag its tail happily, wandering further and further from its master.

Because nothing prepared you, that day, when you were feeling pretty easygoing, for such hostility on the part of your interlocutor, a hostility that left you gasping for breath, and so to-day (even if you'd rather recall some other old minor anecdote instead, such lazy monologues being good for that as well: two parts of yourself, like an old couple, exchanging a few banal remarks whose very banality weaves a certain tranquil familiarity around you, something like a comfortable bath of affection in which you can quietly paddle around; or else dwelling on some other unpleasant event with the aim of finding a better denouement, a better resolution, taking the time, I know how it goes, to imagine some strategy for turning the old scenario around to your advantage) it's *this* event, this one in particular, at once minor and irritating and over and done with, that occupies your thought, stupidly persisting, how can you stop it, and it's pretty much ruining your siesta, the most meager and ridiculous sort of anecdote and yet here it is, capable of provoking a retrospective anger over the fact that you hadn't been able to manage things better, with more panache.

I'm sure, come on now, that you don't have to look very far to pull an episode of this sort from your memory, something that you haven't been able to confide to others, given the tenuous nature of the incident, because they would have laughed, would have made fun of how outraged you seemed, your naive way of getting up in arms over something so slight, and they would have replied, seeing perfectly well that their lack of understanding was bothering you but nonetheless trying to get you over to their side, trying to get you to consider things from their point of view, whereas you were stubbornly resisting, but really it was such a small thing, come on, how can you make such a big deal out of it, they would repeat over and over again, good-naturedly, and their making fun of you, even though friendly, would have dug you even deeper into the distress of your impotent anger, as well as encouraging a vague shame in you over having, in their eyes, and even in your own, so little reason for feeling that way.

I can tell it's coming back to you and that the idea that such an insignificant incident is still capable of outraging you makes you extremely uncomfortable. Just to put you at ease, and even to give you some sense of satisfaction, permitting you to compare that tiny incident still capable of preoccupying you so foolishly with the one that, oh not every day, far from it, but maybe two or three times a year, when I just happen to think of it again, the thought elbowing its way through all the preferable thoughts that might possibly have emerged instead, takes possession of the limelight in my own reveries, which are immediately appalled by such a frivolous emergence, and the incident grows even more offensive because of acknowledging the power it still has to arouse such disproportionate wrath, so that, regarding such a banal episode, you could tell yourself that you, at least, have your reasons, in comparison to the utter flimsiness and unbecoming nature of my own, that thanks to me, you finally feel your rights have been recovered, your prestige restored, that's what I'm here for, a quick dusting off never hurts, because after all you're my guest, gently now, a chamois cloth because your well-being means a lot to me (that's how I am), there you go, I'm working on it, I'm ready to tell you a silly story, one of the silliest, really, the story of one of the many incidents that have irritated me over the course of my life.

Hear, then, the lamentable fable of Christine Montalbetti (so, me, exposing myself to you in one of my most absolute failures), pitted in battle with a tobacconist at an ocean-side cafe whose building takes only the tiniest slice out of the main road heading down to the water, a tobacconist whose features I can no longer visualize (to the extent that if I were to run into him today by chance I wouldn't be in a position to recognize him and resume our fight and perhaps even be able to change his mind), but whose silhouette, emerging from the shadows behind the counter, is definitely rather heavy (without being excessively so, neither fat nor muscular), and who has, I think, a round face, but, again, nothing but generic features (eyes, eyebrows, nose, mouth, chin: all absolutely conventional) are registered there in my memory.

It's summer; I'm visiting friends and, needless to say, not on my guard. I spent the morning in the hachure of a pine grove, then ate a waffle undulating with hills of whipped cream, which cream fell, near the attractions on the promenade, to cover an already chocolate ground with its snow (that's the way my vacations are), I'm relaxed, I'm not expecting conflict, I walk along with a light step to shop for the things that help me collect my thoughts when I contemplate the world around me and maybe when I sit down at a desk, if I feel like it, or maybe on some terrace, but anyhow, I'm feeling pretty happy and not very demanding.

So, as I usually do, I ask for a pack of Gauloises Brunes Extra (that's what they were called in the days that this obviously tenacious story goes back to, now ancient, since they've since been rebaptized), but the person setting the requested goods down on his counter delivered without warning a solid, irrevocable *they'renotforyou.* That is, he didn't address me with an interrogative phrase such as, "Oh, you smoke Gauloises Brunes?" in the tone of somebody who is inquiring, either because he's temporarily taken some personal interest in me, or else in something belonging to me, the precise nature of which he is unaware and in any case doesn't need to be formulated, he's hooked for whatever reason and so wants to strike up a conversation with me and ask about this particular point in my short lifetime and all its modalities, which do concern him after all, since it's the reason for my presence in his territory; or else out of thoroughly mercenary motives, because it's good to make polite, verbal contact with his customers; or else as the result of a more abstract interest, a sociological interrogation for example, him being interested in the fact that there are women—in fact, here's one now—who smoke dark tobacco, and looking for the origins of this oddity in geography, membership in a social group, profession, who knows what; but no, the tone is peremptory, it leaves no room for opposition, there's not a trace of hesitation in the voice, but, chancing it, Here we go, I gamble, I try out an affirmative rejoinder, we'll see if I win, yes, one can allow oneself this sort of small skirmish, nothing at all playful about it, nothing whatsoever, no room for contradiction, no flexibility.

My reply (I maintain flatly that yes, they're for me) doesn't sway him at all. But that's not the end of my troubles. I take out a bill in the currency of that period—this scene, like I said, although very minor, makes for an unpleasant memory, and the obsolescence of so many of its details makes it even more pitiful to know that it was able to leave so indelible a mark in my mind, from which so many more important facts seem to have been erased—and that's when he wins: "People who smoke Gauloises Brunes always pay in coins." He's got his evidence. Just listen to that. And I, what can I do faced with such evidence, so unconvincing that my reality invalidates it, yet supported by what from his point of view are conclusive statistics? Why, I ask you, is it that my situation does not simply constitute in his eyes a first example to the contrary? Why doesn't my presence, my reply in good faith, have the power to make him waver in his vision of the world (and with the result, after all, that he could go home happy in having learned something new to tell his wife and his friends, Hey, you know what, there she was!)?

Go ahead and laugh, that's what this anecdote is for, make fun of my simpleminded irritation and its persistence, yes, relax, that's it, compare yourself to me, find yourself superior, that's fine, come on, perk up a little, good, and our thirty-year-old likewise, fading a bit on his bed, during his tentative, fickle siesta, in which his thoughts sometimes return to the figure of the lonely mule driver, on whom he confers increasing importance among those pictured on the screen, providing him with thoughts that, during his trip, this mule driver would turn over inside his mind, like anybody else, this man who looks deep into the monochrome horizons of the cloth and dreams about the usual insignificant things, while his mule, who knows, might perhaps construct some mute discourse of its own, or why not out loud, prolonging this late afternoon with animal tales, our man returning occasionally in a more melancholy way to the individual riding this talkative animal, the person onto whom he projects himself with more and more certitude, turning him into something like a small graphical double.

Still, nothing that isn't perfectly natural, don't you think, as long as this mule driver trotting in silhouette on the toile de Jouy doesn't turn around and wave at our thirty-year-old, or, worse, as long as he doesn't get down from his mount to come over for a little chat with us, imposing himself without so much as a by-your-leave, coming on his own initiative to where we're sitting to make himself at home on a corner of my desk, sitting himself boldly down on the walnut surface, legs stretched out in front of him, feet at right angles to his body, or on the arm of your chair, which might provide him with a more comfortable perch, especially if it's a rounded armrest that he could straddle like he was his mule just now, letting his legs dangle against the floral motif of the cloth; or else, how should I know, maybe you're lying down and, it would be unavoidable, he'd have to be there at the head of your bed, standing and eyeing you up and down from his great six-inch height, in any event holding his gray silhouette erect and moving around so convincingly as he talks to you that he ends up acquiring some real-world color, just look at that, a bit of red on his cheeks at first and soon, having acquired a real taste for it, his whole complexion begins to go pink, and then his hands, which he's waving around in the air like white doves, at first they turn a beautiful flesh color while he keeps on yakking, and now his clothes don't want to be left behind, the pants turn blue before our very eyes, his shirt stays white and his hair black but now the latter has auburn highlights, and we can see his worn-out shoes darken from the colorless things they were before into a beige hue, down to their rope soles, they're kind of like espadrilles but appropriate to the period, and maybe as he stands there he might sometimes take off one or the other to rub his feet, because they can swell up pretty fast when you're riding a mule, he would explain, trying to excuse what he's doing (and the resulting sight of his tiny toes and his plantar arch, neither of which are, well, immaculate); and probably you would let him know by means of gestures that it doesn't matter much to you what he does, come on, this individual who has so shamelessly entered our universe like this, brazenly taken possession of your armrest as if its ergonomic curve had been made precisely for him, or even perched on this corner of your pillow, wait now, and your old hygienic reflexes return, because really, he shouldn't be allowed to leave sand from his travels on the pillow where you lay your face, it would irritate your cheeks, even sand on his tiny scale, especially since it's a known fact that there are all sorts of not very nice microorganisms scraping out a living in sand, and really it would be disgusting if he dropped some protozoa on your cotton pillowcase, better not even think about it, protozoa that would then scamper around on their pseudopods all over the same places where your lips will soon be pressed, a hell of a situation, and where in the morning you will have spilled a little lake of saliva, something you're quite entitled to spread around since, after all, it's your sleep and your pillowcase.

No, instead, let's just kick this donkey driver right back onto his screen, especially since I can tell, yes, and for a little while now, you've had a perfectly legitimate question in reserve, held back politely, your amazement discreetly contained, because after all, in that scene with Harry, there was, of course, a rather irritating element, many irritating elements in fact, let's run back through them again, so, firstly, the humiliating modalities of Harry's silent refusal, secondly, how our thirty-year-old couldn't get the gun belt he wanted, that always gets on your nerves, and then, thirdly, you'll have no trouble admitting, the fact that you were forced to review this incident rather than see our man's thoughts slip away to more cheerful subjects, because, it had seemed to you, well, anyhow, if you're allowed to formulate an opinion here, you take all sorts of oratorical precautions, you thought that maybe there might be more serious things to discuss than, here you give a little cough, than this matter of the gun belt, and as for me, well, I could whistle to myself, looking like I didn't understand, casual as can be, replying, More serious, well, I don't think so, but I wouldn't be able to stay on this tightrope for long of course, I can't help but agree with you, and it's clear to me that I finally have to get around to telling you a bit more of this sad story.

4

Because, really, and this is the underlying question that was irritating you just now, while you were listening to all my nonsense about the mule driver: just what is this dreadful epic recorded on the gun belt, a few episodes of which Harry read with his fingers?

You have to admit that every story will always harbor a few obscure areas. There are always sequences about which, perhaps, you might not have been unhappy to get wind of some detail, but where a few ellipses have been allowed, and so you tell yourself, fine, that's part of the game. For instance, maybe you want some more information about the scene that took place inside the house between Dirk and Mary, yes, you would certainly have liked to be told that little scene, but, nonetheless, you filled the gap however you could, each according to his own temperament, some convincing themselves that, after all, maybe things weren't quite as spicy as appearances led us to believe, imagining some banal and empty-headed dialogue, Dirk having been so deeply moved by nothing more than Mary's mere brushing past him as she went through the door, sure, sometimes that's enough; others attributing Dirk's amorous turmoil, visible as he was stirring his coffee on the terrace, to the immediate past when a kiss was exchanged within the dark interior of the house, a restrained kiss, due to Mary's fragile, serious temperament, or else, on the contrary, something pretty hot, erotic, with tongues, and maybe even more, who knows what you might be dreaming about, what you imagined could have happened in a corner of the room, to the left of the cupboard I suggested you put there, on a sink perhaps, that would do nicely, with a solid work surface that, though it's a strain, can withstand the weight of a body; or else you led them to the kitchen table with its empty surface onto which Mary could have lain flat on her back, see, or else would have set her elbows, it all depends, and you remember your finest hours—but our thirty-year-old, still outside in the courtyard, didn't know any more about this than you, that's what made you feel better and, no doubt, helped you accept this gap.

But this time it's about our own hero's past, and you aren't prepared to be kept out of it, how disparaging would that be, when you've been accompanying him so willingly all day long, having temporarily set aside your own affairs and even neglected your own friends a little, who also demand that you give them some of your time; and so you feel you have the right to know a little something about the painful past that our thirty-year-old says nothing about, that must come flooding back into his memory at every opportunity and certainly at Dirk and Ted's place earlier, even though he never lets it show.

Okay.

In that case, let's take a look at his past as though it were an adventure story, as Harry rightly understood it, leading us through diverse landscapes, woodlands to start with.

The episode in the forest consists of a long, mad dash through sharp branches that rip the young man's clothing and leave red, burning cuts on his flesh, while his feet get caught in the thousand treacherous roots that, rather than going underground the way they should, protrude in woody convolutions that have no business being outside, so that, stumbling on these adventitious roots, he sometimes falls flat on the ground, bumpy with hard flint-stones and strewn with all sorts of hostile elements, sharp and piercing pine needles, for example, when he doesn't land right in the middle of the common polypod ferns that so generously adorn the undergrowth and that dredge up old fears in him, attributable perhaps to the fact that these Pteridophyta are among the most ancient plants (they were already spreading their deep-cut fronds, speckled with not-at-all-unsavory spores, in the immemorial days of prehistory), and also serve as camouflage for certain snakes whose bite is never exactly desirable.

English oak, Scotch broom, and bladder senna dispute the landscape, and in the midst of this still-vegetative scrawl, blue cedars that seem to lurk here like huge, hairy paws, and then the soft erasures of poplars, some lindens, plane trees defoliating calmly from generation to generation, monkey puzzle trees (a kind of thorny pine that it's easy enough for said monkeys to go up but not to get down again), ashes with black buds in winter, alders dangling male catkins, yellowwoods, bean trees, a few mountain ashes too, every one of them displaying foliage nonetheless populated by such fanatics of defoliation as the lepidopteran caterpillars always drilling their mines, and where sometimes you can see a beech weevil dash by, swift and nimble on its bulbous hind feet—or even, look, some wooly aphids—while the resinous exudations on the trunks of these pine trees no doubt reveal the presence of cochineal beetles causing injuries to the phloem (not to mention the lignicolous fungi sprinkled over their bark, the epiphytic lichens, and other such pleasant gifts of the natural world).

Our thirty-year-old slept, when he let himself sleep, on the ground in hollows he was able to spot and dig out wherever the landscape was uneven, but he ran the rest of the time, eating berries he picked in passing from the raspberry bushes in clumps full of suckers and the floriferous bushes of currants in bunches.

And since his mind was nothing more at this time than a huge black pit with nothing running through it, though just aware enough to diagnose the dreadful condition of its own emptiness, he took it into his head to pull himself together by focusing on one single memory, the memory that helped him survive. It was a memory that, at the same time as demonstrating the kind of family affection he'd once been the object of, also, obviously, could stand as an analogy to the situation in which he now had to live, among the dendrological species, evergreen or deciduous, surrounding him, and which—forked, branching, or mossy, speckled with the little black sticks of frondicolous insects—raised their leaves, framed against the light, in establishing shots of his new home.

Here's what it's all about. The single memory our thirty-year-old had of his childhood at Sevenoaks was the visit of an uncle who had spent a few weeks with them and who, at night after supper, which took place around five o'clock and consequently left a bit of leeway before bedtime, had told him, episode by episode—and like something he had been told by somebody else with whom he was on equally avuncular terms, if I've got my details right—the travels and, I believe, writings of a certain St. John de Crèvecoeur, a Norman by origin, who'd inherited an estate in the neighborhood of Pierrepont (and was "Michel Guillaume Jean" in the registry, rather than St. John), and who—regardless of where he was in his adventures as a cartographer or bookseller, before he then undertook a long sedentary episode as a colonist, and then, after later events that cast him into a life of great solitude—always found writing to be the activity in which he could best converse himself, as he himself described it, rehashing then the vanished days of good fortune. Thus, he did not just write, said our thirty-year-old's uncle, lifting a didactic index finger against the rocky background of the fireplace (whereas the uncle's own uncle must have made this same gesture against a cozier background of a living room with walls striped in pastel blue) a *Traité de la culture des pommes de terre* (Treatise on Potato Cultivation), which of course had its own interest, but also something else, a novel in the English language at first, which became, in his own vastly modified and augmented translation, done on his return to France, a sort of self-portrait, entitled *Letters from an American Farmer*, the farmer being named, in fact, St. John, a novel that, I'll just mention in passing, was quite successful. Anyhow, the thing that the uncle was telling about, suiting the story to his audience, in this case our thirty-year-old as a child, whom he had to impress by means of embellishing his narrative with some vaguely fabulous elements, was precisely the tale of being lost in a forest, a more catastrophic version of which being provided every evening, emphasizing the shadows thrown by the branches and their inextricable entanglement, turning the lost traveler into a poor doomed thing who, eyes fixed on the ground, was looking in the jumble of roots for some small trace that would show him the way, floundering through wooded swamps where occasionally an avocet, a common redshank, or a kestrel would take off into the air. He was hoping with all his might, because he was getting all scratched up in the dense undergrowth, that he would come upon some little sunny spot cleared by the inhabitant of a log cabin who would then invite him in, which is perfectly natural, who would feed the traveler some restorative dish, and whose conversation would stand in sharp contrast to the lunatic silence of the forest.

And this poor St. John (the same one who, studying the eggs set before him on a table, was in the habit of imagining the hens and roosters they could have become), would envision, to spur himself on, a tulip tree with its pyramidal shape adorning his host's garden, and then, rested, he would exchange a few mundane, and then, take it from there, philosophical thoughts with his deliverer, bravely holding forth on the weather, on exile. But no, there were nothing but alders and willows (not necessarily weeping: the white willow, for example) here, and so the man who was lost went on talking to himself insistently in the forest, so he wouldn't lose his vocabulary. Sometimes he would make comments about plants he'd encountered as though he were pointing them out to another person, always including some scientific trivia, regretting that he couldn't glue the specimens into an herbarium, the thought of which would connect him with old memories; sometimes he would sob out loud as he enumerated all the things he would like to see occur, as if his litany—trying perhaps to formulate a desire even nobler than his usual, and thus move some spirit within earshot to pity—might end up making its object appear.

And sometimes he would alternate his despair with moments of renewed and excessive enthusiasm in which it suddenly seemed to him that his wanderings would absolutely have a happy ending, and he would then picture the brilliant shape this finale would take before relapsing into a skepticism just as radical as his fantasies had been blissful.

The clearing that St. John de Crèvecoeur had obviously managed to come across in the end—since one day he had been able to write about his adventure—was finally discovered by our thirty-year-old as well. The clearing in question was moreover graced with a cabin, empty, in which our hero naturally chose to make his home.

He spent several seasons in this clearing, in a life that he could almost describe as domestic, going back and forth between the rudimentary walls of the small cabin and the outside where he found things to eat—an outside with which he now had a completely different relationship, since now, in fact, the outside was not the indifferent, omnipotent nature through which he had to drag himself day and night, but a place to go to with a purpose in mind, often focused on the house itself, its improvement, or on the food stocks he was amassing inside it.

The cabin was very simply furnished, its only contents consisting of a straw mattress, not very springy to say the least, in which a colony of apparently rather healthy bedbugs flourished, and a single wobbly stool, which, the first time our thirty-year-old sat on it, had the annoying habit of letting what turned out to be its rightmost foot slide out further to the right in a completely uncalled for entrechat, throwing our young man off balance so that he found himself flat on his back at the foot of his seat. Remembering the spectacle he must have made and feeling a little silly, he no doubt laughed, something that hadn't happened to him in ages, with a solitary, slightly sour laugh that had some difficulty getting out: a scrawny, feeble laugh, but happy all the same to have emerged.

And this convalescent laugh, somewhat astonished at its own existence, swaying, let's say (well, you know how my mind works by now), on its legs, as it seeks to discover some still difficult-to-achieve stability, brushing itself off so as to look more presentable, ended up staying inside the cabin, moving into a corner from which it carried out its tutelary duties, like a sort of household god if you will, a protective and benevolent Lar, nestled inside a Lararium of its choosing, on a square of natural wood perhaps, accepting the precarious conditions of its life (nothing here of the pediment it might have preferred, the columns it could have demanded, neatly arranged on both sides of its altar), more often than not straddling the roof beam and, from this viewpoint, overhanging the room, sending its happy and carefree waves down to our hero, who, sitting on his mattress, is resting from the day's labors.

Because our young man had very quickly developed a minor Robinson Crusoe-like operation there, making his own tools more or less successfully (I won't mention the attempt at a hammer that miserably disintegrated at the first blow, its fragile joints instantly coming apart), feeling his way along with modest inventions, proceeding somewhat empirically, with, from time to time, an occasional pause in which he would stop and reflect, glancing quickly at the fickle sky and chewing on a stem of bent grass or fescue because such mastication helped him form an abstract and rational picture of the technical difficulty he was then encountering.

Thus we see him spending his days outdoors for the most part, cutting wood and bundling it, going off to fish, by hand at first, locating water holes, trying to catch fish from underneath in the palm of his hand, or, turning over a flat rock, gently, hoping to find a crawfish hiding there, not muddying things up so the water wouldn't lose its clarity, than with a trap put together with reeds to form its framework, having attached a net to it, using braided grasses that he already knew to be supple, or even with a harpoon (a firmly fixed pebble kept the barbs he had cut from a reed spread apart, their points carved to create something like the tongue of a buckle), occasionally busying himself with gathering a few aquatic insects that could be used as bait. He would lie in wait for the trout stationed in its water vein, the midge-catching fish that dwelled under cover of vegetation along the shady bank; he waited for carp, catfish, or doctor fish, lampreys or perch (the latter, for your information, have the reputation of being unpredictably moody).

He would go back through the clearing with his catch, enjoying the bracing effects of a cool, fresh breeze (did you know that, in the woods, wind-speed is slowed to eleven percent of its force in the open air?), occasionally stopping to track a Canada goose flying by against the bright sky like something carrying a thought, a little thought fluttering there, all befeathered and weightless.

And sometimes he would stay with this thought a bit—thought for its own sake, abstract, detached from any practical considerations—to process it, advancing cautiously through the hazy backdrop of other ethereal ideas, somewhat unsteadily, treading silently, every sound sucked in by the cushioned ground, puffy and flocculent as snow, over which these thoughts introduced the long specter of their vague, black silhouettes, sketched in against all this nebulous white.

Then he would start back down the path towards the cabin, beneath a sky sometimes hanging overhead like a painted fresco, sometimes with clouds moving along at their own pace in a rhythm affording him the pleasant sense that the day was passing him by. Yes, occasionally there were swift skies whose fluid, cursive contours gave you the feeling that you were being left behind, right? as if, yes, it was all going on up there without you, in a different temporality than your own, and its great celestial speed left you exhausted.

In the evening, seated in the light from the hearth, beneath the satisfied gaze of his Lar, which had a necessarily foreshortened view of him, compacted down to just head and thighs, essentially, our thirty-year-old would take sustenance, then stretch himself, in either a strictly brachial extension, or with his legs as well, since they instantly demanded attention, accompanied by the slight sonorous emissions that signified his contentment, and which came to lodge themselves in turn on the wooden square already holding his protector and thus forming all sorts of ever-more-numerous little Lares around our man, the souls of the stretches that had taken place in this room night after night, and so in time this makeshift altar began to have quite an impressive look to it.

One day, however, he had to leave the clearing.

It couldn't have lasted forever anyway, of course, this reclusive life, in which, his talents as Boy Scout having been exhausted, all that was left for him now was to repeat the same mundane tasks he'd perfected, stuck in the materiality of everyday things, benefiting only himself; but an event hastened things.

To explain: our man had, during one of his flights of wood-working fancy, constructed a table, pretty good for an amateur, not the least bit wobbly, and with a hint of personal style that did no harm at all, which he had placed in front of the rectangular gap in the cabin wall serving as a window and through which in the morning he would contemplate the pretty progression of light on the meadow as he drank his cup of hot water infused with some herb brought back from his walks (I'll spare you the system of rainwater collection that he had invented).

On this table, following a sudden decorative urge, he had placed the sole piece of dishware other than the cup that he had found upon arriving at the cabin: a small jug on which, painted in blue, there was a picture of a hovel standing in front of a line of fruit trees on a little hill.

Said small jug (should blame for the proceeding occurrence be placed on chance, the weakness of the adductor muscles in a bird's beak, or maybe—no hypothesis should be excluded—a meteorite that might have exploded quite a distance from the cabin but that, alas, let a minuscule rock fragment fly off with such great speed as to exacerbate its density; or should one, in fact, see a human hand in this, and, well, then what? was the piece of pottery an accidental or, indeed, a willful target? and in the second case, was it a completely capricious event, a piece of harmless mischief, or a warning, really, leading you to believe that our thirty-year-old might just have an enemy?) on a day that had, despite what was to come, begun in a perfectly ordinary manner, was hit by a splinter of flint-stone that burst its china walls apart, ruining, you saw this coming, the design of the painted shack, now in pieces on the table, while the dwarf pear trees that formed its background hedge had erupted onto the floor.

Our man cast one last glance on the scattered pieces of the destroyed shack, filled the leather flask he had sewn together the preceding winter, and resumed his travels.

What comes next is woods and forests, the passing seasons, snow returning to stick its white fluff on the walker's clothing and cover the landscape with white powder, rivers and going down them in rafts that our man fabricated using the trunks of poplars and on which he navigated the best he could, shading his eyes with his hand or pushing a pole against the bottom, with a few episodes of splashing that it would be pointless for me to enlarge upon.

Until one afternoon when, suddenly emerging on foot into a pass from which a grandiose vista where the multiple strata of successive levels of vegetation lay stretched out in front of him, he saw below, dark, projecting its copious smoke vertically, but also laterally in two gray moustaches that lifted in the breeze, *the iron horse*, as they called it. Introducing the locomotive.

Confronted with anything for the first time, you know, one must make a wish. Our hero was seeing a locomotive for the first time. He made a wish. His wish came true. Two days later he was in a freight car.

He had himself contributed to the realization of this wish, because it's always a good idea to help things along a bit. He had gone down into the valley, had walked to a difficult section of the track where it seemed logical that the train would have to slow down, and since the next day's train had, in fact, slowed at that spot, our man, after first getting a running start, had jumped into the freight car, hop, through its half-open sliding door.

Sitting down on the floor in there, amidst the clumps of straw and other hard-to-identify waste, his legs folded like the underpinnings of an insect, giving him a slight orthopteran, acridian air, cricket-like, he had scarcely turned his eyes to look outside when his retinal rods and cones were entirely overwhelmed by the sight presented them, doing their best to grasp the abstract, fluid shapes of the parts of the landscape flashing through their field of vision.

Those blurred lines, some of them broken, gradually became the image of a world that, once one had successfully focused on and then deciphered and identified those vague lumps, those spots, those unclear areas, seemed to be moving on its own, since our man's body, thank you very much, wasn't performing any muscular activity. Thus did our hero learn his first harsh lessons concerning the relativity of movement, it being fully expressed in those potent tracking shots permitted by the train—whereas on the raft his thoughts had focused more on coping with liquid and mineral dangers than on how the landscape was going bouncing by in modest leaps.

Our man was thrown ever so slightly off balance at first, because after all, this process demands some small reorganization of the visual cortex, also probably of the cognitive zone that's connected with that particular area. But then, as with anything, one eventually adapts, and he finally ended up covering thousands of miles this way, with the result that soon the poplars, the pines, the wild apple trees emerging more and more clearly for him and without his having any trouble at all, visually, with regard to them, were succeeded by the fantastic silhouettes of cacti that had scribbled their often shriveled initials against the sunny background, some of them rather like wildly branching pilasters, others tubby and juxtaposing the disks of their paddles against one another in an assortment of peculiar arrangements.

He continued this initiation into their bizarre alphabet up to Rough Rock Junction, where he decided it would be good to stop. In payment for some odd jobs he had done at Jefferson and Co. Ranch he acquired a horse (I'll skip the economic details of the transaction) as well as a Smith and Wesson that he hooked onto his old belt, and soon he had taken to the road again on his equine acquisition, stopping off from one village to the next, sometimes for months at a time, until he had finally arrived right here.

Ever since (since that time), he's gone upstairs every day to take a nap in this room, shuffling small ideas around as described, closing the strings of the wineskin holding the sleeping memory of his long epic starting with the catastrophic departure from Sevenoaks as tightly as possible, lying back and letting any future peripeteia in his story arrive entirely of its own accord.

5

Which apparently it does. Because just take a look at what comes next.

The acoustic space of our thirty-year-old's siesta is torn, as it terminates, by the polyphonic arrival of the stagecoach—this happens twice a week—whose axles always work a bit loose in their hubs (bass notes: something like *la do la do re la do),* and then the rims themselves, I don't have to tell you, screech on the ground (treble notes: *si mi si fa si fa mi),* while the passenger compartment rattles (in a minor key: something like *fa fa re fa fa re,* with accompanying sharps), and the baggage bounces around on the top deck (briskly, like clipped eighth notes: *do mi do mi fa re sol).*

The eyes of our thirty-year-old, surfacing from his earlier, opaline daydreams, again take stock of his room, while, at the same time, his mind translates the significance of this acoustical incursion, which tugs him by the shirt, pulling him, as usual, to the window, since, in these small western towns, it's always a good idea to know how many people get off the stagecoach, and likewise to have some early warning as to who they might be, if you value your life.

Another part of his mind puts up a bit of resistance, though, telling the first, Easy, easy there, the stagecoach hasn't even come to a complete stop yet, begging for—what—an extra half minute? so his body can prepare itself, psychologically, so to speak, to call upon its apparently still-unmotivated muscular mass.

At last, the negotiation completed, using one arm as a lever, the other to swivel, our thirty-year-old goes over and hides his face in a fold of the curtain, yes, looking through its lacy open-work, just in time to see the coach driver, Adam Bullock, jump down and go to open the door of the passenger compartment.

Adam Bullock has a story too, of course, like anybody else, but I don't know how prudent it would be to immobilize him—one hand just starting to remove his hat, the other on the door handle—in order to tell it to you right now, given the relative urgency of the situation, which you'll come to appreciate soon enough.

So, Adam Bullock, after a freeze-frame only lasting a few seconds, completes his movement, drawing large half circles in the air with his hat to signify a cordial greeting, pretty proud of himself for having brought all these people here in one piece, so that the poor piece of headgear waved every which way must be feeling dreadfully nauseated and it's no wonder that it soon flops over like some frightened animal having been subjected to the Tilt-a-Whirl at a fair.

As for the passengers, getting out one after another, well, let's see.

The first one, whom I would classify as belonging to the order Batrachia, has a broad, flabby, and swollen face with a hole in it like a valve, as though that was where you put the hose to inflate it, this orifice lined with two reddish lips, skin punctuated with wart-like yellowish beige excrescences, probably inflamed by the heat of the journey and indicative of nothing good, a stocky silhouette, wide at the shoulders, shrinking at the waist to end in two unexpectedly flimsy legs, how much more ridiculous can I make him? how about a little feet-together jump out of the passenger compartment (though without the trampoline effect you would expect from an alert frog) to land abruptly and sink almost an inch into the ground and then, stuck there, his looking like an allegorical statue of Journey's End—but no, let's go, get a move on, the person behind him in the coach is letting our batrachian know that he himself has every intention of getting out into the air and has no problem simply ordering the latter out of the way.

For his part, this second man, telling our batrachian to move it, belongs most likely to the marmoset species, yellow eyes like circles of felt, a wrinkled face, a quite noticeable degree of auricular and brachial pilosity, taller than average, why that's Ralph Tyrrell, and our thirty-year-old, who hadn't even noticed he'd left town, instantly berates himself for this negligence, worrying that he's becoming soft, less vigilant, and shoots Ralph a particularly intense stare, simultaneously indicating his surprise at seeing Ralph thus reappear, some vague guilt over being unaware he had left in the first place (though recently, mind you, because only day before yesterday . . . but skip it), and, finally, the level of renewed concentration our thirty-year-old will now force himself to apply from here on in.

Next one out, an old alligator—can't put anything over on him. His complexion is as dried up as some fossilized Pompeian's or even a multithousand-year-old Pharaoh's, big snout, only a few teeth, but these are pretty sharp, you'd rather not mess with them; that's Joe Alabaster, who edges onto the sideboard with a reptilian sway of the hips but stops short, an old pain reemerging because the nervous, muscular, and skeletal structures at work in his chosen maneuver have been caught off-guard.

This bestiary-trio disperses very quickly, the old alligator preferring to go straight home while the abovementioned marmoset and the anonymous batrachian go off, side by side, each with his own particular gait, to the saloon.

In sharp contrast to these three zoomorphic figures, the next-to-last passenger presents us with the profile of a handsome leading man, but it's too late, thinks our thirty-year-old, who's occupied the center of this story too long to be dethroned by this new young man—apparently about seven years younger, in good shape, with black hair, blue eyes, you have to admit he would make a good-looking lead—who goes by the name of Jonathan Weaver, a fact that we might ourselves be able to learn later on, in some roundabout way, but which our man is as yet unaware of, making an instantaneous assessment of how quickly Weaver's tight, elegant body would be likely to draw a gun, and then the resulting ballistic precision, taking notes further to a brief psychological portrait, for instance—in the plus column—the kid seems nice enough, but, also—in the minus—we all know that naive and impulsive young men wearing gun belts are likely to touch off any number of catastrophes, even with the best intentions in the world.

Once on the ground, our handsome young stranger turns to look back inside the stagecoach and offers a humble forearm, willingly turning this part of his body into a simple support, a handrail, a bit of dutiful wood, letting it become a nobody, forgetting all its amazing accomplishments, its wonderful skill with a gun, no, it's just an object now, a transitional piece of furniture onto which our thirty-year-old—watching through the mesh of the curtain that haloes the whole scene in white—sees a gloved hand place itself, while a foot likewise extracting itself from the passenger compartment lifts the hem of a dress so that the skirt's fabric arches out from the knee; then the flared top of a wide-brimmed hat sails out ahead of everything else, and it's only when the entire body has found its footing on the ground that its head lifts, hands busily smoothing out her dress, no, I'm dreaming, Georgina Littlejohn.

IV
the duel

1

Georgina Littlejohn.

Our man, whose face was allowing itself to be whipped by the cotton cloth of the curtain flapping in the evening breeze, leaves the window frame, rushes to the washbowl, pours water from the pitcher into it, and then scoops the liquid up in his hands to bring it to his reddening cheeks.

The sort of thing you do on the bank of a river.

The water slips between his fingers; it has the ability to be, in essence, an elusive substance.

Two molecules of hydrogen for just one of oxygen, as everybody knows, clinging so tightly to each other that together they shy away from everything else, always aiming for the interstices of the man's hands where, finding an easy egress, they make a break for it in their wavy fashion.

The molecules regroup, stream off, and like paratroopers arrive together at the edge of a finger, evaluate the space separating this finger from the next, and then off they go, they jump, they fall back into the bowl where they rejoin the great crowd of their peers, once again forming a single, larger substance with them.

The whole thing takes place as if, by means of some sort of magnetism, the molecules actually wanted to be back in that bowl again with the others, reintegrating into the medium from which they had been extracted, as if we were dealing with a kind of . . . well, *alien*: a single, large, fluid entity, elastic, that can survive being pulled to pieces, is able to be separated into distinct droplets, a divisible entity in short, but one still alive in all its separated units, so that each time they're taken apart, a genetic program leads them to reunite, to seek to regain, in any way possible, no matter how far off they may have strayed, how far apart, how cut off from the rest, their original association.

Of course, they don't all succeed in this enterprise, and some start to evaporate, perfectly awful, leaving behind—where they split off and disappear—scarcely more than a microscopic calcareous remainder, a white trace that is invisible to the naked eye but is rather like a little skeleton, mmm, meaning they did exist.

Others, defeated by the cloth of his shirt, let themselves be absorbed by the fabric onto which they've drifted by mistake, falling there, having aimed poorly, having taken a leap in the wrong direction, or else finding themselves knocked off-course as they fell by some unexpected gesture, for example, intercepting them. In their free-for-all with the material now imprisoning them, their first strategy is to stain the textile, making its color darker, that way notifying you of their presence, their mingling with its cotton threads, more fragmented than ever, clinging in infinitesimal bubbles to the lianas of this braided material, hanging on to their little ropes, unable to do more than await a certain end.

Unless . . . their little hope-filled brains still tell themselves "unless" as they sway back and forth on the string they're gripping between their arms, clasping it as closely as possible in order to maintain maximal adhesion. But it's not terribly clear what could save them, except, perhaps, a washing, where, since the whole shirt would end up in the bowl, they could loosen their limbs from the fabric and, making a quick escape, swim off again with their fellows however they see fit, simply focusing on the fact that they shouldn't let themselves get caught anywhere near the piece of clothing later when it's finally taken out of the bowl, because then, like a net, it will carry off a good number of aqueous molecules, these doomed, inescapably, to dry up, probably on the back of a chair (though one can always imagine a backyard, where the heat of the sun would further speed their extinction).

The likelihood that our thirty-year-old would choose this precise moment to wash his shirt, when his thoughts seem to be attending to completely different matters, is obviously almost nil, however, and so the molecules still in the bowl must now mourn those of their comrades presently dispersed on his shirt, where the natural friction of the air will surely be the end of them.

Sometimes too, in their failed trajectories, the drops fall onto skin, there to engage in a little duel with this surface, impermeable for the most part but not entirely, because the epidermis, happy to have this very local, very unexpected hydration, may greet them with the appetite of an ogre, with the result that the molecules will soak into it in spite of themselves, restoring a bit of lubrication to the dried-out upper layers, becoming one of their constituents, enslaved, absorbed, readapted, torn away from themselves.

Invigorating the parched cells that, otherwise, would certainly have cracked, exfoliated, fallen off in translucent scales at the least abrasion, they give up their former freedom, now the servants of these same cutaneous units, which they will irrigate for a time before perishing along with them in ever-progressing and inseparable desiccation.

This is true of the arms, anyway, where the skin is relatively arid, but on the forehead, on the cheeks, the water molecules, aided in their escape by their great numbers, their flow, washing along at the mercy of facial bone structure, more like torrents, a landscape of little waterfalls, probably gravity too is involved, aiding them in their return from exile, encouraging them to return to their place of origin, our molecules are not, by contrast, sucked in almost immediately, since here the skin is already exuding some moisture of its own, letting beads of sweat like little bubbles out through its widening pores.

They then enter instead into competition with this product of the sudoriferous glands, an organic liquid with a high content of eye-stinging sodium chloride that makes our water molecules turn aside, holding their noses, trying to open up a path that will let them get away.

This diaphoresis, by the way, has obviously been provoked, I'm getting to it, by feelings brought about by our man's vision of Georgina, and then, you've already guessed, fed further by the memory of a specific episode, flickering in visual strips, you might say, across the inner screen of his thoughts, where they alternate with erasures being caused by the efforts of his hands, still dispatching little slaps of water, trying to dilute the too-thick, too-severe, almost blunt memory of it all; but his eyelids, in spite of themselves, when they close against the splashes, form a good surface onto which he can project a few images of the scene now wafting back to him.

Before I tell you about it, though, you might be happy to know that at the very moment our thirty-year-old is splashing on his face the labile water escaping as a result through his fingers, Samuel Frère, back in the Old World, is finishing the last page of his *Mémoires d'une goutte d'eau, ses voyages et ses transformations à travers l'air et l'eau* (Memoirs of a Drop of Water, its Journeys and Transformations through Air and Water), then, getting up from his work table, permitting himself a beneficial lengthening of both arms in the direction of the moldings on his ceiling, and accompanying this with a happy moan, together signifying work completed, fatigue not in vain, and the relaxation produced by stretching, goes out for a short stroll in his garden, where the green trees, the stormy sky, and invigorating wind all serve to perk him up again.

He has just closed his folder on a first-person tale in which a drop of water recounts the emotional turmoil of her very busy existence. Readily conversing with the other drops of water that she encounters and that provide her with information on the state of the world, informing her about the phenomena taking place all around her (she finds that her interlocutors all make reasonable statements that just so happen to add up to scientific explanations of all the beauties she perceives), and warning her whenever necessary, she turns out to be quite a polyglot as well, communicating just as easily with a fossil pebble (Jacques

Boucher de Crèvecoeur de Perthes, hero of one of my earlier novels, *The Origin of Man*, would, I assure you, have been delighted by the scene) as understanding whatever human conversations might be going on nearby.

Born as vapor (that is, still "a small, elusive, absolutely empty globule"), she became fog (calling herself a vesicle at that point), then, finding herself forced into too small a space with numerous other drops, all of them fighting over what little room there was to spread out, arguing over the way-too-circumscribed territory where they'd all wound up, she finally, caught in a storm, falling to earth, landed on a snowy mountain, and, after taking a good look at herself, ended up baptizing herself "drop of water." From this point on she led a life full of didactic adventures, occasionally punctuated by some small talk, for instance when she runs into a drop of water that was one of her friends, and, traveling with her in a river current, watching the banks go by, they babble and chatter, yes, just look at those two gossips talking about everything they see and replacing the earlier pedagogical discussions with little babblings of amazement.

It just so happened, however, that our drop of water would soon withdraw into more secret preoccupations. Deep inside, she reflected on her state with some anxiety. Absenting herself from the conversation, she tossed about, yes she did, new lines of thought, sometimes bitter, sometimes happy, constantly reasoning with herself, trying to be happy about the rustic nature of the countryside, but with something a little forced about all her delight, which nonetheless almost convinced her in the end. And when, panicking over being so fragile and so small, she wavered at the thought of her own existence (comparing herself, one day, to the vastness in which she'd been absorbed, she found the comparison unfavorable), she quickly told herself it wasn't worth dwelling on, told herself she must be mistaken, and found this made her feel better, she was a good soul really, succumbing to her own arguments, letting herself soften, but always capable of poetic enthusiasm, a truly brave little drop of water, I'm telling you, always going forward, not letting herself get all worked up, and, if some metaphysical thought came to mind, quickly getting rid of it, as though it were some midge, like, there you go, you give a quick oar-stroke with the back of your hand in the air, see, just to send the pest packing. Feeling some regrets, delicate nostalgias, letting her mind wander in sugary dreams, the drop of water always found herself quickly absorbed in new adventures that would distract her from her tendency to brood.

The sudorific recollection of the episode in the barn at Seven-oaks, because that's where we were, and because we can already come out and say that the incident being recalled also took place in a barn, has very little to do, of course, with the details of the setting, which one could nonetheless go to great lengths dis-cussing, how it was arranged, for instance, the first sight of the exterior barnyard once you go past the oblong drinking trough that, because it's constructed out of beams, like a boat, looks like it's waiting to be launched, and where a few members of some eccentric species of gallinaceans are pecking away, odd because their copious plumage goes all the way to their feet, making them look like they're wearing bellbottoms that need hemming, since they get all tangled up, they're always stepping on themselves with disastrous results, forcing out a few clucks; partridges and grouse meet up there as well, but we're going to set aside this avian digression, I can tell it's not really your thing, alas. And as for what's inside, plenty of straw, yes, dancing around in the sectioned light projected by the high windows, introducing a rather majestic chiaroscuro effect with a sophisticated photonic architecture that contrasts with the obviously rustic theme of the décor as a whole.

The painful part of this, I'll tell you right off the bat, has to do, for starters, with the sight of his then-skinny chest, which Georgina, methodically unbuttoning our hero's shirt (at the time we're talking about he was something like fourteen or fifteen), had revealed with its sunken sternum where the xiphoid appendage looked like a blade engraved in the watermark of the skin. The puny adolescent, in order to make the scene bearable, imagined that this was his nurse beginning to undress him in order to make him put on different clothes, letting her do it, as if he were merely a coat hanger with his shirt on it, holding his shoulders very straight, concentrating on being a good coat hanger, as if what was going on concerned him only distantly.

You can probably see a bit better now where I want (or don't want) to get from here. The elusive water, rippling sweetly on our thirty-year-old's cheeks, but always giving him the slip, in no way keeps him from repeatedly recollecting this moment, even when that other drop of water, Samuel Frère's, insists on shoving her way forward to tell everyone about how—having been carried one day, despite herself, through a pipe—she found residence in the pool of a paper mill, then in its boilers and vats, and finally in its presses, and indeed about her opinions on papermaking methods, an activity in which she was proud to participate (she remembered too how once, while swimming in a fountain, a schoolboy had put her into his bottle and then had spilled her accidentally onto the pages of a history book, whose stories she had then read eagerly).

Georgina, finished with the unbuttoning, had stopped what she was doing and seemed uncertain for a moment, as if hesitating over whether the part of her project pertaining to clothing held any interest (the boy, for his part, was stubbornly pursuing the notion of her being his nurse), as if she'd noticed, for example, that she had no change of shirts to offer him, a notion the brain of the terrified child now clung to, no hand yet having touched his visible bone structure to linger eventually in the valley of a clavicle where his skin, more delicate than elsewhere, would finally offer Georgina's uncertain fingertips the satisfaction of a *locus amœnus*.

There were even more tribulations in store for our literary droplet, however: in the mouth of a river, for example, in hopes of soon seeing the sea, she managed to get scooped up in someone's bucket; then he threw her into the barrel he was carrying on a cart drawn by Norman horses, and then from the barrel into a watering can so that she eventually fell on the stalk of a heliotrope that wasn't doing very well. She fed the flower through its roots, lodged in its stalk, was carried away with it from the garden a few days later and then put in a flowerpot placed on the tablecloth of a ceremonial dinner at a house in the city. When one of the lady guests, gazing pointedly at the heliotrope, congratulated the host on the decorations, her neighbor broke off the branch containing our drop of water and held it out to her. Instantly the lady stuck it into her hairdo. Then, as this woman was going home, probably at a happy and vivacious pace, our drop of water fell onto the pavement and, swept into the gutter the next morning, returned to the Seine whence the man's bucket had scooped her up a few days earlier.

Our thirty-year-old, continuing with his ablutions, takes a taste of the water, starts gargling, thinks better of it, spits it back out, unaware of how Samuel Frère, in my place, would have been inspired by this to begin the terrifying tale of these spatterings from mucus membranes and expulsions into the bowl (Georgina now, in turn, like a young woman getting ready to dive in after God knows what from the banks of a river, had undone her blouse). Whereas our thirty-year-old, still mixing this fresh water with the salt water he's secreting, skips ahead, remembers what happened further along in the scene, you can probably guess, I mean, I don't necessarily want to go into the rather intimate details of what went on, you yourself are perfectly able, sorry, to project your own memories of losing your virginity onto all this (you can dream away comfortably, put this book down, cover open like a soaring bird, gliding wings widespread—is it flying over the meadows of the flowered armrest that I ventured to imagine a little bit ago when I put our impudent mule driver on it, or else is your armrest made of corduroy, resembling furrows in the bare earth, or is it the dark, nocturnal ether of the cloth of your pants we should be talking about, where this book looks like a wild goose catching a glint of moonlight, or else the whitish sky of your sheets, where our goose will spread out its wings the way it would on a gray day?).

The fact remains that, at the end of their bucolic frolics (ever practical, when it had the opportunity; the writer from Rouen's drop of water took a particular interest in drainage systems, and irrigation methods weren't foreign to her either: distribution into secondary channels, headraces, bucket wheels, none of that intimidated her; in a more epic vein, however, she also never blushed to mention battles with powerful octopi, their victims subjected to the stranglehold of tentacles with dreadful suction cups; and, when poetic, our chronicling drop of water could also describe the motion of tides, their ebb and flow, the moon's gravitational effect, and so forth), Georgina returned home, feeling, if nothing else, the persistence of the full, living shape inside her, which sensation would accompany her for a bit in her daily farm tasks; and our little, brand-new young man, running over and over the event in his mind, had likewise left the barn.

Finally drying his face in the sponge-like cotton of a towel that he gently presses to his skin like a compress, forcing away the blood beneath because of its pressure and leaving pale, fleeting traces before the vessels irrigate it once again, our hero glances quickly in the mirror lying behind the bowl, then, disappearing almost immediately from the surface of the silvered glass, he cuts this self-portraiture short and leaves his room.

2

All at once, entering a saloon, you find yourself endowed with the optical capacities of the most vigilant of drosophila. These bugs, we know, are equipped with faceted eyes, which must, one imagines, be very useful when, thrust into an uncertain environment, and having premonitions as to its vaguely hostile character, you want to have a panoramic view of it, without necessarily losing, as you turn your head, the sight of what had just now occupied your field of vision, because, becoming erased as you turn, it can always change while unseen to include some new element, which would, in that case, elude you at the very moment that it possibly begins to constitute a threat.

In reality, of course, things are probably more complicated than they seem, concerning drosophila. Ommatidia are set in a rounded shape, tending to multiply the angles of vision, so that, probably, the shape of an object falling through the cluster of lenses finds itself considerably elongated. Looking into the works of our scholars, we see that Muller, for his part, around 1826, and hence a little earlier than this scene, put forward the hypothesis of a mosaic model: each ommatidium would be responsible for a minuscule portion of the image, and the overall vision would thus be formed from the juxtaposition of these fragments, which wouldn't be so bad, really. But there are also naysayers who claim that single lenses have a much better reputation for being able to resolve a complete image (and vertebrates of course make use of exactly this system—might we detect a touch of self-congratulation here?), so that, according to them, it's not impossible that these small creatures have a rather blurry vision of the world. But, let's just make do with the vulgate version, okay?

So I present our hero to you now as a dipteran, who, as soon as he went into the saloon through the two swinging doors with their blinds and springs (boing boing), each giving the warm, early evening air a good slapping and sending great shovelfuls of its substance on their way, had, with his ever-ready musciform gaze, grasped the composition of the group scattered there around the room, assembling an exhaustive list of them in no time at all, a list we ourselves can now spend some time examining, because we're not unhappy, at least I hope you're not, to be back again in this little group of people, people who are beginning (this is always an emotionally gratifying process) to become familiar to us.

We first notice the animallike duo who, obliged by their species' incompatibility, are now separated: the batrachian of the pair having set himself down at a table, motionless as a china toad, pot-bellied and placid, on a doorstep, and the marmoset, answering to the name of Ralph Tyrell, having remained standing because of his chronic bipedalism, leaning against the bar where, from time to time, he scratches the cutaneous areas that a siphonopteran is targeting one after another.

Among the individuals that we met as we walked to the ranch earlier on, we'll certainly recognize Will Nordman, always preoccupied, gazing deeply into a canvas in his mind showing a meandering landscape where he seems to imagine taking a walk (because, yes, when you want to get away from the situation you're in, from the bar, you can always imagine taking this path lined with its wild hachure of grasses, envisioning the lands hiding beyond those hills, the lands one will soon reach at long last), while Jeff W. Dunson, seated beside him, turns his converging pupils toward the insides of his palms as best he can, with the beam projecting from his right eye and that from his left converging at point A", between points A and A', where each of them, respectively, was intended to strike.

Jim Hopkinson, we understand, had to stay home, perhaps still sitting in the shadows watching for the silhouettes of the people who can't get to the saloon without going past his house, which is to say, primarily, Dirk and Ted Lange, right? who are certainly here in the saloon, ah yes, Ted, good old Ted, already talking up a storm at the bar, buttonholing that marmoset character on who knows what subject, which, however, he left hanging when our thirty-year-old came in, taking time to greet him from a distance, and Dirk too, likewise standing, but slightly in the background, his gaze surfing along the mirror over the bar and splattering in its reflections whose bursts of light, overexposing his retina, drive him to a steady palpebral squinting, this still being the best means of protecting oneself from such. John Burns too inevitably passed by Jim Hopkinson's windows to reach the bar, but I don't see him, oh yes I do, slightly hidden by Dirk, seated on an isolated chair, his interior monologue apparently a thousand miles away, on a bumpy sled, surveying some snowy domain, if you ask me.

Thomas Burnett, being someone who had no need at all, given his topographical situation, to submit his person to the ophthalmic sweep of the fiendish Hopkinson, displays a complete, though somewhat sketchily traced silhouette, and not having thought it a good idea to interrupt his conversation on account of our thirty-year-old, continues to ask Adam Bullock a few polite questions concerning his recent trip. The latter, more than willing to be questioned, answers with pleasant anecdotes, and also, from time to time, with an encouraging touch of his hand on Howard Nelson's arm—Nelson no longer looking so unhealthy because he's spent the day resting—making him join in.

Somewhat obscured by the shadows, where he hides his black eye, Richard Evans is no longer feeling at all aggressive towards Nelson, and is willing to pose with him as a mere extra, leaving stardom for anybody else who wants it tonight, on the principle that it's perfectly normal for them all to take turns.

We might also mention the presence of Sam Buckeye, whom you haven't met yet, and whose unpredictable temperament prevents our always knowing in advance what he'll do next, and then Ben Cottonwood too, whom Sam is sitting with, but Ben is a nice guy, nothing to fear from him.

As for the horrible Harry, is he absent tonight, no, there he is, seated at the end of the bar and raising his eyes toward the newcomer to favor him with a Hello Stranger that's still vaguely ironic, before plunging back into the contemplation of the entwining of his remarkable fingers, which he seems to be braiding into a coil.

Behind the bar, Morgan Perry is filling glasses, turning around occasionally to take a bottle out and, while his hand digs around in the cupboard, casting a glance at the room duplicated in the mirror over the bar where the doubles act just like their masters, with perfect servility, imitating them without ever making fun, reproducing their gestures in a choreography that looks off by just a tenth of a second—in the realm of reflections, all movement seems forced, as though compelled by some tyrant, since we have never, in living memory (or am I wrong?), seen one of our duplicates falter or daydream, lifting a hand later than us, or else facetiously beginning to pick its nose while we still have our hands together, and when we think about these poor slaves, their will broken by the totalitarian mechanics apparently forcing them to obey, we can see that we have, I believe, gotten the better deal.

You take advantage of this reverie to take a look at the saloon's furnishings, as well as at how the room is laid out, because, of course, you had already begun to picture the place when those three friends of ours were remembering last night's brawl, but it's quite a different thing to find yourself here in person. You put your hand on a wooden chair and lean on the back of it so as to further examine the few mismatched round tables scattered around from here to the back door, to the left of which you recognize the rectangular window with the worn linen curtain that you didn't know it had, flapping like a rag mop around this opening into the dirt yard.

A picture draws your attention too, the portrait of a man with a cast in his eye, some sort of squint-eyed ancestor of these locals, whose strabismus flows from one two-dimensional face to the other, from the original painting to its reflection in the bar mirror, a man who, erect in his fitted coat, like his twin located in the glass, wearing the same bright orange scarf whose lively color is a little shocking in this context, continues along with his double to listlessly supervise these nights at the bar via their no doubt distorted vision of things.

The chandelier's copper arabesques, descending in a graceful tripod, each end fitted with a small spinach-green cup made of dull glass and shaped like a fluted bell, despite their graphic complexity, are reflected just as easily as anything else, this reflection simultaneously complicating the trajectory of the light particles arriving to bounce off the mirror's glass and, without the least effort, increasing their number.

But it's time to get back to our scene, where Jonathan Weaver remains to be mentioned, because, standing with his back turned three-quarters of the way toward our thirty-year-old, he too must have been letting his attention wander around the room he's just entered for the first time, with a gaze that, though synthesizing all his impressions at first, then became content to drift from detail to detail, following a rather disjointed optical trajectory, slowing down over two or three elements as they haphazardly presented themselves to his field of vision, emerging from the background, perhaps revealed by the play of light, requiring his eyes to halt, momentarily, in virtue of who knows what secret, tacit affinities—more often than not—or else, on the contrary, entirely obvious examples of distinctiveness that certain elements of scenery offer up and that make such and such an object (such and such a form, shadow, or material) appeal to you more than some other as a result of some closeness or strangeness, it's not always explicable and would be pretty hard to argue with, and anyway is probably loosely connected to your own story, pieces of which you drag around with yourself and occasionally make an effort to remember, though these elements aren't the only thing in your environment, there's also the silent mass of all the other items that just don't catch your eye, an anonymous and insistent crowd demanding attention that you refuse them and seeking retribution for this slight by means of all sorts of tiny, ill-defined, pernicious revenges. Anyhow, associations of this sort, the origins of which remained mostly obscure, had provided the rhythm to Jonathan's panoramic shot as it slowly checked off the items in the saloon, making its last stop on the surface of the mirror, where it rested a moment (the reflected eye traps the actual eye so quickly that it would be impossible to tell which of the two acts first, the simulacrum or the real organ) before detaching itself from its replica, in a synchronous release, to pivot towards the newcomer: let me present our thirty-year-old. So, our man, his gaze catching the outline of Jonathan's silhouette at the same instant, can't help but recognize there, alas—astounded, in fact, by such obvious evidence—the young man he might have been, the young man whose ghost, sure enough, must therefore weigh heavily on our scene.

For, in this person now accompanying Georgina—did I forget to mention Georgina?—with proudly unbridled subservience, in all the antithetical impulses driving his contradictory personality—the Baked Alaska component of his character, so to speak—how could one help but see a sort of anachronistic double—I make this assertion without stressing it—an incarnation, one can't help but think, of the transitional young man who under normal circumstances should have come into being between the puny child who first discovered Georgina's body in the barn and tonight's thirty-year-old: yes, the one who should have embodied this evolution, the precise form he should have taken back then, rather than the wandering figure he had been in reality, to fill in those intermediate days.

Our man doesn't linger over this idea, perfect and crystal clear. He simply pans across the scene nostalgically. The image he takes in, instantaneous, sharp, and precise, doesn't require detailed examination; it's the kind of vision that's indisputable, like those enormous revelations whose details are unimportant because, being so overwhelming, they have the power to convince you that they've left nothing out, that they are entire, that their significance will brook neither contradiction nor modulation. Here, says this spectacle, is the young man you could have been if only . . . driving the bitter blade of this hypothetical history deep into the heart of the man contemplating it.

Our thirty-year-old abandons this vision almost immediately— the poisoned offering just made to him by Jonathan who, just a few yards away, makes a painful display of its veracity by means of his body, his posture, his breathing—to, last but not least, as they say, turn toward Georgina.

Georgina.

The Velcro effect is instantaneous. The adhesive capacity of Georgina's gaze is immeasurable and their retinas immediately grip each other—we all but hear it, don't you think, crackle, the hook side and the loop side leaping together, their complementarity joining them instantly.

Or, rather, between this woman's two pupils and those of our thirty-year-old, two cords, let's say, have just been stretched, having the circumference of said pupils and containing within them all sorts of information now circulating with astounding speed, information so dense I'm not going to try to disentangle it, their common past at Sevenoaks flowing there like lava, mixing into its powerful, composite flood all sorts of shards, yes, shards, as if this woman, shaking herself, had scattered all sorts of corpuscles into the room, fragments originating in the old days, flying toward our thirty-year-old, splattering on him before he could think of bothering to protect himself from them.

To which must be added this bizarre detail: Georgina's intact appearance, her fantastic resemblance to herself, which shakes our thirty-year-old up a bit. Because, not content with setting off this otherwise perfectly normal flow of memories, wherein the straw of the barn flies around through the shafts of light traversing it, Georgina herself seems to have stepped this very instant out of that day at Sevenoaks, somehow teletransported, from the barn of his childhood into the saloon, in defiance of chronology, as if only the setting had changed.

If you think about it, this feeling, which one really does experience sometimes, including when it comes to people with whom one's relationship had been distant and not, strictly speaking, emotional, who, when seen again fifteen or so years later, seem to be absolutely congruent with the image that our memory has retained of them, far from provoking some despondent acknowledgment in us of the deleterious passage of time—legible right there on their faces and creating in reaction a little, egocentric, worried impulse, the fear that, contemplating us in turn, they might be making exactly the same observation—arousing, on the contrary, the notion of a sort of eternity, or anyway a lasting quality, incomprehensible at first, this sensation, I maintain, if you go into it a bit more thoroughly, can be explained using a simple mathematical calculation.

And, in fact, despite all the changes that have doubtless, without our noticing the effects, afflicted the details of their skin, on which dry winds have certainly blown, making little wrinkles appear, or accentuating the grooves already in place; despite each person's personality having been remodeled as a necessary result of the events of their life, no matter how stoically we may have faced them, stiffening our little selves because we want so much for them to be monolithic and unchanging, faithful to prehistory, needing as ever to draw some founding hypotheses from them—unless, of course, we did quite the opposite, lowering our heads at the first sight of trouble, taking off haphazardly for part unknown, until we frequently lost sight of ourselves despite the yoohoo-yoohoos we sometimes tried shouting after us to set things right (so that we ended up by stopping and asking ourselves as we contemplated the slow parade of clouds across the countryside, projecting their moving shadows like big autonomous splotches onto the mountains and valleys, why we always had to be our own prodigal son)—finally, in spite of all these changes, of skin or what lies beneath it, there is, nonetheless, one element that has certainly not progressed in the least, a rational, calculable element, namely, think carefully about the different parameters involved, the age gap between our hero and Georgina, who is his elder, that is, the temporal element that separates them. Or doesn't separate them, but always stands between them, and always to the same extent, like a constant bond, even if this gap might seem elastic to you for one reason or another (if you think, and it's your prerogative, that not all years have the same weight; if you think, for example, that one particular year can count double, while another counts for nothing). This is the perpetual, mathematical gap that is the secret of Georgina's glorious identity with herself.

Kept thus at this same temporal distance, which extended between them like the little red plastic stick connecting two molecules in those science model kits, a little stick that allows them to spin around against the navy-blue background of space without the gap between the two of them ever varying, Georgina and our thirty-year-old are also bound together in our saloon by the aforementioned cords extending from their pupils, and it's now time for us to get back to them.

You know those rope bridges that sway above steep mountain passes, or perhaps over a river of knotty rapids whose gray waves swell to harrowing effect, well, this is the sort of structure that our thirty-year-old now undertakes to cross, while Georgina contemplates his progress proudly from the other bank.

Her silhouette is motionless aside from one tiny quivering point, it's that mother-of-pearl earring hanging from her earlobe, trembling, a tear-shaped object, a small, vertical, opaline shell, its delicate turbulence not easily attributable to any one particular cause: is it merely the inevitable, infinitesimal momentum of being alive, the continuation of her pulse, which must certainly be bringing blood to the lobe, beating at the spot pinched by the earring, its jolts making the bead attached move as well; or the effect of some emotion, because only the acceleration of her otherwise perfectly normal circulation, only her pulse's actually racing, you decide, could justify so much bead-swinging, some sort of contained but widespread trembling in her pouring out via its oscillations; or else, wonders the scientific mind, should we perhaps see in the pearl's slight twirling a further proof of the earth's rotation (*e pur se muove*), visible if you think about it in all the pendulous motions to which our small, constantly turning world is subject—because you sometimes envy your peasant ancestors who, after a day of working in the fields, contemplated to the sound of the Angelus the flat stretches of land caramelized by glowing light and then went off to sit very peacefully dusk after dusk, their chairs set securely in the dirt floor where their feet, digging in slightly, found them a comfortable position, with the undisturbed notion in their minds that this is how things were for the entire world, a single great surface, completely level and motionless, perfectly horizontal beneath the same sky.

This tremulous bead encapsulates the room reflected therein, vaguely deformed by the roundness of its pearly surface, with, in its center but without detail, the slender, elongated, drawn-out, blackish figure of our thirty-year-old.

To him, time seems distorted, slowed down, as he moves toward Georgina. And though all kinds of memory images are fighting tooth and nail for his attention, though he is experiencing any number of contradictory feelings, these elements are not waging their wars on his face, turning it into a chaotic battleground, every nerve, every muscle for itself, racing here, vibrating there, tumultuous, incompatible, messy, no, instead they've been choked back to the level of his stomach, leaving his face smooth, expressionless, like a placid ferryman resigned to the fog through which he is steering his boat.

Yes, that's it, our thirty-year-old is crossing a stream, a river, he moves his oar with the slow, sure movement of someone who's made his way through this saloon many times before, compensating for the thick and widespread fog that is his lot on this crossing with the knowledge he has of this so-frequently-surveyed space, with the physical memory he has of this watery landscape where Georgina's opaline earring, like a delicate moon still capable of piercing through this fog, sends out the light luring this ferryman on, snapping him up, captured by its whitish halo.

And while the saloon continues its anamorphosis on this mother-of-pearl surface, our boatman, determined and lanky, continues moving along, feeling his way slowly toward the ceruse light. It wouldn't take much for us to hear the water slapping beneath his oar. See how, by the sheer strength of his stubbornness, he has almost reached the shore. How he is preparing to throw the limp mooring line toward a tree now appearing out of the fog. The rope zips through the air in a loose coil then catches on its trunk. Natural as can be, the man pulls on this rope, hand over hand, and so brings the boat closer to the shore, shortens the distance, hauls his craft to land.

He steps onto the shore, scarcely inches from this tree, and now, hey, listen, apparently it can talk, because he's scarcely drawn level with it when the sizable plant (of course I'm talking about the woman we've already discussed, in her satin dress) begins to open lips that you probably imagine to be full (and you're not mistaken), painted (you're not wrong), deep red (you're really good at this), showing, that's right, tiny, pearly teeth.

Two words now reach our ferryman's eardrums (Georgina's eyes are so close to his now that, despite the weak light dilating her pupils, he can confirm the presence in her irises of the vaguely ligneous semicircles that he had always seen there in the past, resembling the duramen in the cross-section of a tree trunk), hopping, like storybook toads, out of Georgina's mouth.

What they are is a first name followed by a last name, two monosyllables, less than exciting, and right away you can tell that they absolutely do not refer to our thirty-year-old, but are, rather, informative in content, pretty disagreeable, concerning a third, in fact very unpleasant party who might already be in the vicinity and whose arrival Georgina had come here to warn him about, having heard, who knows how, where our thirty-year-old was living, and not hesitating (or else her own internal monologues on the subject simply haven't reached us) to take the stagecoach here as soon as she learned what was happening. She had brought Jonathan with her, who knew nothing about any of this, but was willing to follow her unquestioningly, more than happy that she was allowing him to stay by her side, offering her the protection of his arm, which was always willing to be considered an inanimate object when she might have use for it, serving as an occasional table, banister, even a cane when she wished, a polyvalent and articulated arm, a natural appliance, very convenient on trips. Jonathan, devoted and proud, had been able to swallow all his questions, reserving his anxieties for those moments when he was alone, picturing the faint horizon of some secret that would know when it was time to come out, telling himself that she would reveal it when she felt like it, as he carried her luggage to the coach before offering her his forearm, which, you see, Georgina, he seemed to say, in the fluid, harmonious, perfectly appropriate gesture that he then executed, you can always count on.

The monosyllabic first name immediately followed by a last name of the same length treading on its heels like an inspector setting out to tail someone, peremptory, leaving little breathing room between, this duo, that is, of a swaggering first name and the authoritarian patronymic that never lets it out of its sight, hangs in the air for a moment, like a figurine dangling from the rearview mirror inside a car.

Then our thirty-year-old's mind anticipates the imminent deed that he must be ready to carry out, or at least the first stages of it. Like lightning he sees three shots of himself: leaving the saloon pronto, the leap he'll make to mount his horse, and how he'll gallop past the nearby edge of town.

And he does indeed carry out these operations (since, in any case, you're already way ahead of him, imagining that the duel providing the title for this section of the novel would pit our thirty-year-old against some young, porcelain lead, all of it over some woman, of course), after having thanked Georgina with a flutter of his lashes and without waiting around a moment longer, because there's also a lot more being said in Georgina's eyes, stuff she's having difficulty holding in, the part of herself that would have preferred to keep quiet about that name, for instance, and then her fear, her anxiety pouring out about how this sequence of events will be resolved, not to mention her sorrow, gasping now over the dangers that our man is preparing to face because of her revelation—and we shouldn't remain transfixed in that sort of look—am I right?—if you want to get on with the action.

The dreadful name, which may not mean anything to you, but that you will never forget, is Jack King.

3

We are standing now at the precise moment of intersection, the crossroads where day, in a long fade, lets night win out, opposing it with thoroughly inadequate means, really, in a battle lost in advance and vaguely troubling to the heart.

With each return of evening, as long as we're standing by a window, or else outdoors and consequently making the association between the chromatic display and the sensation of increasing cold, even if just the coolness of a summer night, doesn't the scene make us feel a sort of discouragement over the loaded dice at work, weariness at the certainty of the outcome, which isn't necessarily the one we'd want, because we prefer bright skies, the natural light that comes slanting into rooms, outlining all kinds of shadows on our walls, faint, diluted, calligraphic, among the large, overexposed rectangles, sometimes eaten away by a figure, the corner of a shutter, or a piece of furniture that, intercepting the photonic projection, gnaws into an angle, making the exhibition even more fantastic.

We understand, how could we not, day's resistance to night; we'd like to offer it some support, if only we could; we add to our regretful feelings of empathy for it a sense of our own powerlessness, faced with this sky utterly overwhelmed by the advancing invasion of bilious pigment and yet mobilizing itself however it can in small pockets of brightness, doomed to failure of course; we are truly embarrassed to be present at this futile battle, this great massacre of what were, just a moment ago, healthy, lively photons.

Without mentioning that we have, what's more, a very poor opinion of ourselves, worthless and idiotic there under the darkening sky.

The aperitif, someone explained to me recently, as she put some breadsticks weighed down with marbles of salt onto a low table, was invented specifically to distract one from this sight (ink was rapidly soaking into the garden, it was time to begin shelling the pistachios).

Yes, but what to do when you're urging your horse on, I ask you, into the now-deserted plains, with all the urgency of a mission that must be accomplished?

Tonight we have one of those wildly striped skies where the most vermillion of reds clashes with pale orange, where even old rose manages to insert itself from time to time, incompatible with the high yellow content of the rest of the tones, the whole thing (red, orange, jarring pink) scratching across a background of rather electric gray; you have to admit that the results aren't in the best of taste, but it's clear, in all this chromatic fury, in these stripes, these scarifications of the celestial flesh displaying its open wounds, in these painfully twisted reddish filaments that look almost like bits of flayed skin fluttering in the evening wind, it is clear that the sky too is joining in the coming violence.

Yes, the sky that could have spun a lovely, amaranth moiré for you is instead offering these crimson tatters, flapping like gruesome banners.

And it is beneath just this twisted, scarified sky, darkened with coiling clouds, motley and vaguely ominous, that our man gallops his horse.

The name of Jack King fell like an enormous weight onto the other end of a seesaw, so that our thirty-year-old, sitting on the near side and daydreaming, till now, with his feet on the ground, had been sent, right then and there, hurtling into the breeze.

The name, far from having started him off on some long interior monologue on the subject—developing it point by point then proceeding cautiously to consider the ways he might respond to this terse bit of information, finding in the cultivated field of his reflections, which would have called upon all his rational capacities, the route most appropriate, the conclusion following most naturally from this long sales pitch—had set him instantly into motion. In fact, everything went ahead as though it were a matter of immediate—though, thus far, you certainly must have noticed that our thirty-year-old prefers to wallow in temporalities that are really quite luxurious, that are mostly made up of lots of waiting around—and instinctive response, a reaction that hadn't taken a path through thought at all, as if the auditory stimulus of the name had instantly sparked the action of the muscular mass required for turning on his heels, propelling his body out of the saloon, then onto the rump of his horse, which had apparently been waiting for exactly this moment, a powerful animal into whose flanks he is now persistently digging his heels.

The still erubescent sky lays its coral reefs around dark stretches of water. Above the bare countryside, grayer and grayer, bristling here and there with the infrequent whitecaps of a few frizzy, steppe-biome bushes, whose wooly balls crumble beneath the tread of pitiless hooves, a second landscape unfurls, one that looks fantastically maritime now, and things that should really be described in terms of oxygen and nitrogen, I'll spare you the details, degrees centigrade, luminosity, the spectrum, well, you translate it all as creeks, peninsulas, shining seas, desolate harbors.

You drift off a bit into the marine setting painted for you by the glossy clouds up in the ether, the parallel fiction of crenellated banks, in some places boldly irregular, in others blurred by coastal fog, gripping dormant, oily waters in haunted shores.

The stones on these shores, reddish, are certainly volcanic, so there's also the lingering threat of imminent eruption, capable of destroying the dark, tenacious, petrified shores' configuration, giving way before a scree of broken rocks swept along by the wild lava that would carry them farther afield in complete chaos.

The name Jack King is like a pulse of blood, pounded out by the hooves of the equine specimen now galloping at top speed, it fills all the thoughts of this man making his horse run and run beneath the rubiginous sky, where what were previously rocks now prove to be scrap iron, stained with long, powdery splinters of rust, things don't seem to be working out too well.

And, if you were to study it more carefully, you might have to describe it, this extremely flushed sky, as blotchy with rosacea, though even that wouldn't be sufficient, rubicund maybe, that's not quite it, afflicted with roseola, you're getting there, because, anyway, there's something about this mottled, pimply tissue that's pathological, you can't deny it, you're diagnosing a dermatosis, you're afraid it'll spread, turn into a major case of psoriasis, against which background, remember, our tiny man is riding, you go back to your hypothesis, you're worried about this excoriated skin, it's really not encouraging, look at those oozing edemas, those scales and blisters, yes, you decide the sky is eczematous, and you're quite right.

Finally the silhouette of Jack King makes its appearance beneath this erythrosine-smeared sky.

He is cantering toward the setting sun, probably having planned to wait until it was completely dark before setting foot on the ground and lighting a small fire in his solitary encampment where, all alone, he would be able to think through his sad affairs, mull over his bizarre and terrible thoughts.

But this itinerary will have to be amended. For, as our thirty-year-old lengthens, if such a thing is possible, his horse's stride, and shrinks the distance separating them, although this is still sizable, Jack King becomes aware—is it the particular way the ground trembles, or a sound wave bouncing back to his ear despite the racket of his own horse's hooves and the screeching of the air being split, like a sheet being torn, around him; or else just the intuition of a man always on the lookout—that he is being followed by another rider, likewise alone, he has no need to turn around to know this, and is still far enough away that the simple remedy of urging on his mount, which is far from moving at a full gallop, is still conceivable.

But Jack King wouldn't say no to a bit of fighting in all this dreary desert. And if he left a certain question up in the air—the question, that is, of the identity of the person in pursuit, which later would circle like a hard-to-identify vulturine creature, sometimes soaring in a troubling circular pattern, with the threat of its curved beak always overhead, sometimes flying away again, but not without first reminding him that it could come back at any moment, transforming, don't you think, the texture of time with its comings and goings, since its absences wouldn't represent any kind of respite, nor a point at which one could redirect one's thoughts elsewhere, but a gnawing pain, in fact, since one's mind would be occupied the entire time in imagining the moment when the ugly bearded vulture would come back to show its bare neck letting eek! the pink flesh there embossed with hair follicles show; and even if Jack King would do his best to sweep it out of his field of vision with wide, real waves of his hands, wouldn't the bird simply draw wide circles up in the air to let him know that the game still isn't over? In short, this small bird of prey, this insistent question, sure to walk its sharply clawed feet around in his mind later on, look, might as well nip it in the bud, kill the chick in the egg, Jack King tells himself, preferring not to leave the question alone to develop abstractly (the list of candidates who might be out for revenge is too long for him to hope to discover an answer using reason alone) but instead to confront the reality of the situation just like that, and as quickly as possible, in order to make short work of it all.

So he does an about-face.

Against the blood-streaked sky, he reins in his horse, which is astonished at this sudden halt, this turn, and grows restless in the dusk.

To the eyes of Jack King, our approaching thirty-year-old is still nothing more than an imprecise figure with unfamiliar features. He tries out a few hypotheses pertaining to recently encountered people, but none of their bodies fit with this shadow advancing at a trot now, with its whipped topping of horsehair sweeping the red and black stripes of the scenery—while the indented contours of the rocks manage to cut into a landscape that seems, yeah, about to be ripped to shreds by those same dark masses, their sharp peaks making the sky bleed.

Having eliminated the most recent cases, one by one, not one of them matching the present silhouette, Jack King digs, as methodically as possible, through the preceding years, so as to get a slight head start, knowing perfectly well that, sooner or later, this figure will be close enough for him to recognize it.

He examines the preceding years in reverse chronological order, the situations involved in each, and from every fight scene, each scene of slaughter he's managed to perpetrate, he exhumes the memory of those targets who might have gotten out alive, then carefully applies this image to the silhouette of the rider coming toward him. Not one of them matches. There's always some under- or overflow, here or there: a different balance between shoulders and chest, a different way of holding himself.

Jack King keeps going. He's seven years back now. He remembers everything clearly, tries to make the contours of those insubstantial bodies superimpose over this one, and as he takes stock, always fails.

He starts on the eighth year. The sky is growing darker and darker, the silhouette that he's working so hard to interpret begins to merge with its surroundings, despite the fact that it's getting larger as it approaches, thus erasing some pieces of information as it makes others clearer, on the subject of its saddle, for example, the sort of stirrups it's using, which now catch two or three flashes of dying light.

Nine years back, and still nothing that relates to the present situation. The unidentified rider, now no farther than a hundred or so yards away, gets down from his horse.

So: a man on foot, whose hips and naturally bowlegged shape are visible, whose way of walking can be examined, but Jack King is ten years back now, and no one walks like that.

Jack King, who could, it's true, kick his horse into a gallop, destabilize the pedestrian with its speed, knock him over maybe and then wave his revolver down at him, a high-angle shot, instead imagines a brief duel according to the rules, there's nothing else to do, after all, in this desert giving way before triumphant dusk, and that's why he leaps down from his mount which then goes off to nibble bushes and, as far as it's concerned, loses all interest in the question.

So now there are two men on foot, striding across the cracked earth beneath a hemorrhagic sky.

Jack King—his tread unsteady, like that of a man who's been on horseback for too long and so can feel the ground, which his reason knows is fixed, leap up underfoot like a living animal—begins on the eleventh year in his thoughts.

Facing him, our thirty-year-old: wearing his old gun belt, the one that that dirty stinking Harry hadn't wanted to take (we would have preferred a better-equipped hero), but believe me he looks just fine, moving his slender body, which nonetheless fails to resemble any from Jack King's twelfth remembered year.

This much is certain: these two individuals are getting closer and closer to each other. Jack King is still fighting not to stagger on the ground, suppressing his vertigo, countering it with the haughty self-assurance that he's always got handy, though, as far as arrogance goes, he did manage to leave behind the superior point of view assured by his horse, the better to contemplate the world at a man's level, perhaps.

The thirteenth year goes by with as little yield as the previous ones.

A mere few dozen yards separates them now. The equivalent of a very broad river on whose banks they soon come to a halt.

Legs wide spread. Each right hand hovering over the butt of a revolver the way a falcon prepares to swoop down and carry its prey off into the air.

Shot: Jack King, against the light, face completely dark, but that's certainly Jack King.

Reverse shot: in one final, slow burst, the sky, done with reddening now, lets a shaft of amber, flavescent light filter through and light up the face of our thirty-year-old directly.

At that point the fourteenth and fifteenth years drop away, and Jack King, lacking a full set of teeth but still with a good pair of lungs in his chest, laughs a huge laugh that spreads out across the open countryside where there are no vertical surfaces to stop it.

"Whitefield," the syllables are buffeted in the spasms of laughter now fading away in a long acoustical death: "Christopher Whitefield."

Hearing one's name spoken in the dusk closing in on this desert plain, after not knowing it, not thinking it for the past sixteen years, well, I don't think you can imagine what that's like.

A blizzard of unheard-of magnitude, a cyclonic wind ripping everything apart, an atmospheric phenomenon churning at cataclysmic speeds, because yes, on hearing his name our thirty-year-old is struck by a past hurricane, an enormous wave, a ground swell, everything he has tried with all his might to hold inside, pushing in the fragile wooden door he had tried to close against the flood of memories, the door he'd constantly had to reinforce by any means possible, only letting slip by, once in a while, after it had shown its credentials, some nice, happy memory of Sevenoaks, or else, oozing in no matter what he did, between the laths, so to speak, the episodes that had followed his forest escape, the resulting epic, but the event itself, which had triggered this uprooting from Sevenoaks, no, never, he had locked it down inside with his name, pushing it all down with all his strength, and now, here, here along with the name, this event too is released, all its accompanying images, those of the house at Sevenoaks, how this man, Jack King, had burst into that house, the terrible carnage he hadn't hesitated to inflict there, in cold blood, and the dreadful sight, repressed until tonight, when it revived with Jack King's laughter, the dreadful sight of his mother's body, falling beneath a rain of bullets, with her blue apron, flour still on her hands, and the body, it's not over yet, of his little sister, falling the same way, she who a moment before had been sitting on the floor playing tea-party with a bowl now splattered with her blood, and through the front door, squeaking back and forth, half-open, on its hinges, after Jack King's departure, his father's body, flat on its stomach, the first killed, face down in the garden soil.

Our thirty-year-old's hand (how many hours had he hidden there, under the bed, before escaping toward the forest) suddenly swoops onto the butt of his Smith and Wesson.

In a tenth of a second he fires on Jack King, who, still laughing, barely even grabs for his revolver, then collapses on the sand.

Whether due to precaution, insistence, or a purely mechanical reflex, Christopher fires a second time before blowing on the barrel of his smoking gun and putting it back in its holster. Rather calmly. He walks slowly to his horse, takes it by the bridle, mounts it, and rides off into the setting sun, against which colorful background, how could it be any other way, his silhouette grows smaller in peaceful accord with the laws of perspective.

A novelist, playwright, literary critic, and theorist, CHRISTINE MONTALBETTI is also a professor of French literature at the University of Paris VIII. She has written five novels.

BETSY WING is a writer and translator whose fiction collection, *Look Out for Hydrophobia*, appeared in 1991. Her recent translations include works by Assia Djebar and Paule Constant.

SELECTED DALKEY ARCHIVE PAPERBACKS

Petros Abatzoglou, *What Does Mrs. Freeman Want?*
Michal Ajvaz, *The Other City.*
Pierre Albert-Birot, *Grabinoulor.*
Yuz Aleshkovsky, *Kangaroo.*
Felipe Alfau, *Chromos.*
   Locos.
Ivan Ângelo, *The Celebration.*
   The Tower of Glass.
David Antin, *Talking.*
António Lobo Antunes, *Knowledge of Hell.*
Alain Arias-Misson, *Theatre of Incest.*
John Ashbery and James Schuyler, *A Nest of Ninnies.*
Heimrad Bäcker, *transcript.*
Djuna Barnes, *Ladies Almanack.*
   Ryder.
John Barth, *LETTERS.*
   Sabbatical.
Donald Barthelme, *The King.*
   Paradise.
Svetislav Basara, *Chinese Letter.*
Mark Binelli, *Sacco and Vanzetti Must Die!*
Andrei Bitov, *Pushkin House.*
Louis Paul Boon, *Chapel Road.*
   My Little War.
   Summer in Termuren.
Roger Boylan, *Killoyle.*
Ignácio de Loyola Brandão, *Anonymous Celebrity.*
   Teeth under the Sun.
   Zero.
Bonnie Bremser, *Troia: Mexican Memoirs.*
Christine Brooke-Rose, *Amalgamemnon.*
Brigid Brophy, *In Transit.*
Meredith Brosnan, *Mr. Dynamite.*
Gerald L. Bruns, *Modern Poetry and
   the Idea of Language.*
Evgeny Bunimovich and J. Kates, eds.,
   Contemporary Russian Poetry: An Anthology.
Gabrielle Burton, *Heartbreak Hotel.*
Michel Butor, *Degrees.*
   Mobile.
   Portrait of the Artist as a Young Ape.
G. Cabrera Infante, *Infante's Inferno.*
   Three Trapped Tigers.
Julieta Campos, *The Fear of Losing Eurydice.*
Anne Carson, *Eros the Bittersweet.*
Camilo José Cela, *Christ versus Arizona.*
   The Family of Pascual Duarte.
   The Hive.
Louis-Ferdinand Céline, *Castle to Castle.*
   Conversations with Professor Y.
   London Bridge.
   Normance.
   North.
   Rigadoon.
Hugo Charteris, *The Tide Is Right.*
Jerome Charyn, *The Tar Baby.*
Marc Cholodenko, *Mordechai Schamz.*
Emily Holmes Coleman, *The Shutter of Snow.*
Robert Coover, *A Night at the Movies.*
Stanley Crawford, *Log of the S.S. The Mrs Unguentine.*
   Some Instructions to My Wife.
Robert Creeley, *Collected Prose.*
René Crevel, *Putting My Foot in It.*
Ralph Cusack, *Cadenza.*
Susan Daitch, *L.C.*
   Storytown.
Nicholas Delbanco, *The Count of Concord.*
Nigel Dennis, *Cards of Identity.*
Peter Dimock, *A Short Rhetoric for Leaving the Family.*
Ariel Dorfman, *Konfidenz.*
Coleman Dowell, *The Houses of Children.*
   Island People.
   Too Much Flesh and Jabez.
Arkadii Dragomoshchenko, *Dust.*
Rikki Ducornet, *The Complete Butcher's Tales.*
   The Fountains of Neptune.
   The Jade Cabinet.
   The One Marvelous Thing.
   Phosphor in Dreamland.
   The Stain.
   The Word "Desire."
William Eastlake, *The Bamboo Bed.*
   Castle Keep.
   Lyric of the Circle Heart.
Jean Echenoz, *Chopin's Move.*
Stanley Elkin, *A Bad Man.*
   Boswell: A Modern Comedy.
   Criers and Kibitzers, Kibitzers and Criers.
   The Dick Gibson Show.
   The Franchiser.
   George Mills.
   The Living End.
   The MacGuffin.
   The Magic Kingdom.
   Mrs. Ted Bliss.
   The Rabbi of Lud.
   Van Gogh's Room at Arles.
Annie Ernaux, *Cleaned Out.*
Lauren Fairbanks, *Muzzle Thyself.*
   Sister Carrie.
Juan Filloy, *Op Oloop.*
Leslie A. Fiedler, *Love and Death in the American Novel.*

Gustave Flaubert, *Bouvard and Pécuchet.*
Kass Fleisher, *Talking out of School.*
Ford Madox Ford, *The March of Literature.*
Jon Fosse, *Melancholy.*
Max Frisch, *I'm Not Stiller.*
   Man in the Holocene.
Carlos Fuentes, *Christopher Unborn.*
   Distant Relations.
   Terra Nostra.
   Where the Air Is Clear.
Janice Galloway, *Foreign Parts.*
   The Trick Is to Keep Breathing.
William H. Gass, *Cartesian Sonata and Other Novellas.*
   Finding a Form.
   A Temple of Texts.
   The Tunnel.
   Willie Masters' Lonesome Wife.
Gérard Gavarry, *Hoppla! 1 2 3.*
Etienne Gilson, *The Arts of the Beautiful.*
   Forms and Substances in the Arts.
C. S. Giscombe, *Giscome Road.*
   Here.
   Prairie Style.
Douglas Glover, *Bad News of the Heart.*
   The Enamoured Knight.
Witold Gombrowicz, *A Kind of Testament.*
Karen Elizabeth Gordon, *The Red Shoes.*
Georgi Gospodinov, *Natural Novel.*
Juan Goytisolo, *Count Julian.*
   Juan the Landless.
   Makbara.
   Marks of Identity.
Patrick Grainville, *The Cave of Heaven.*
Henry Green, *Back.*
   Blindness.
   Concluding.
   Doting.
   Nothing.
Jiří Gruša, *The Questionnaire.*
Gabriel Gudding, *Rhode Island Notebook.*
John Hawkes, *Whistlejacket.*
Aleksandar Hemon, ed., *Best European Fiction 2010.*
Aidan Higgins, *A Bestiary.*
   Balcony of Europe.
   Bornholm Night-Ferry.
   Darkling Plain: Texts for the Air.
   Flotsam and Jetsam.
   Langrishe, Go Down.
   Scenes from a Receding Past.
   Windy Arbours.
Aldous Huxley, *Antic Hay.*
   Crome Yellow.
   Point Counter Point.
   Those Barren Leaves.
   Time Must Have a Stop.
Mikhail Iossel and Jeff Parker, eds., *Amerika:
   Contemporary Russians View the United States.*
Gert Jonke, *Geometric Regional Novel.*
   Homage to Czerny.
   The System of Vienna.
Jacques Jouet, *Mountain R.*
   Savage.
Charles Juliet, *Conversations with Samuel Beckett and
   Bram van Velde.*
Mieko Kanai, *The Word Book.*
Hugh Kenner, *The Counterfeiters.*
   Flaubert, Joyce and Beckett: The Stoic Comedians.
   Joyce's Voices.
Danilo Kiš, *Garden, Ashes.*
   A Tomb for Boris Davidovich.
Anita Konkka, *A Fool's Paradise.*
George Konrád, *The City Builder.*
Tadeusz Konwicki, *A Minor Apocalypse.*
   The Polish Complex.
Menis Koumandareas, *Koula.*
Elaine Kraf, *The Princess of 72nd Street.*
Jim Krusoe, *Iceland.*
Ewa Kuryluk, *Century 21.*
Eric Laurrent, *Do Not Touch.*
Violette Leduc, *La Bâtarde.*
Suzanne Jill Levine, *The Subversive Scribe:
   Translating Latin American Fiction.*
Deborah Levy, *Billy and Girl.*
   Pillow Talk in Europe and Other Places.
José Lezama Lima, *Paradiso.*
Rosa Liksom, *Dark Paradise.*
Osman Lins, *Avalovara.*
   The Queen of the Prisons of Greece.
Alf Mac Lochlainn, *The Corpus in the Library.*
   Out of Focus.
Ron Loewinsohn, *Magnetic Field(s).*
Brian Lynch, *The Winner of Sorrow.*
D. Keith Mano, *Take Five.*
Micheline Aharonian Marcom, *The Mirror in the Well.*
Ben Marcus, *The Age of Wire and String.*
Wallace Markfield, *Teitlebaum's Window.*
   To an Early Grave.
David Markson, *Reader's Block.*
   Springer's Progress.
   Wittgenstein's Mistress.
Carole Maso, *AVA.*

FOR A FULL LIST OF PUBLICATIONS, VISIT:
www.dalkeyarchive.com

SELECTED DALKEY ARCHIVE PAPERBACKS

LADISLAV MATEJKA AND KRYSTYNA POMORSKA, EDS.,
  *Readings in Russian Poetics: Formalist and
  Structuralist Views.*
HARRY MATHEWS,
  The Case of the Persevering Maltese: Collected Essays.
  Cigarettes.
  The Conversions.
  The Human Country: New and Collected Stories.
  The Journalist.
  My Life in CIA.
  Singular Pleasures.
  The Sinking of the Odradek Stadium.
  Tlooth.
  20 Lines a Day.
ROBERT L. MCLAUGHLIN, ED., *Innovations: An Anthology of
  Modern & Contemporary Fiction.*
HERMAN MELVILLE, *The Confidence-Man.*
AMANDA MICHALOPOULOU, *I'd Like.*
STEVEN MILLHAUSER, *The Barnum Museum.*
  In the Penny Arcade.
RALPH J. MILLS, JR., *Essays on Poetry.*
MOMUS, *The Book of Jokes.*
CHRISTINE MONTALBETTI, *Western.*
OLIVE MOORE, *Spleen.*
NICHOLAS MOSLEY, *Accident.*
  Assassins.
  Catastrophe Practice.
  Children of Darkness and Light.
  Experience and Religion.
  God's Hazard.
  The Hesperides Tree.
  Hopeful Monsters.
  Imago Bird.
  Impossible Object.
  Inventing God.
  Judith.
  Look at the Dark.
  Natalie Natalia.
  Paradoxes of Peace.
  Serpent.
  Time at War.
  The Uses of Slime Mould: Essays of Four Decades.
WARREN MOTTE,
  Fables of the Novel: French Fiction since 1990.
  Fiction Now: The French Novel in the 21st Century.
  Oulipo: A Primer of Potential Literature.
YVES NAVARRE, *Our Share of Time.*
  Sweet Tooth.
DOROTHY NELSON, *In Night's City.*
  Tar and Feathers.
WILFRIDO D. NOLLEDO, *But for the Lovers.*
FLANN O'BRIEN, *At Swim-Two-Birds.*
  At War.
  The Best of Myles.
  The Dalkey Archive.
  Further Cuttings.
  The Hard Life.
  The Poor Mouth.
  The Third Policeman.
CLAUDE OLLIER, *The Mise-en-Scène.*
PATRIK OUŘEDNÍK, *Europeana.*
FERNANDO DEL PASO, *News from the Empire.*
  Palinuro of Mexico.
ROBERT PINGET, *The Inquisitory.*
  Mahu or The Material.
  Trio.
MANUEL PUIG, *Betrayed by Rita Hayworth.*
  Heartbreak Tango.
RAYMOND QUENEAU, *The Last Days.*
  Odile.
  Pierrot Mon Ami.
  Saint Glinglin.
ANN QUIN, *Berg.*
  Passages.
  Three.
  Tripticks.
ISHMAEL REED, *The Free-Lance Pallbearers.*
  The Last Days of Louisiana Red.
  The Plays.
  Reckless Eyeballing.
  The Terrible Threes.
  The Terrible Twos.
  Yellow Back Radio Broke-Down.
JEAN RICARDOU, *Place Names.*
RAINER MARIA RILKE,
  The Notebooks of Malte Laurids Brigge.
JULIÁN RÍOS, *Larva: A Midsummer Night's Babel.*
  Poundemonium.
AUGUSTO ROA BASTOS, *I the Supreme.*
OLIVIER ROLIN, *Hotel Crystal.*
JACQUES ROUBAUD, *The Form of a City Changes Faster,
  Alas, Than the Human Heart.*
  The Great Fire of London.
  Hortense in Exile.
  Hortense Is Abducted.
  The Loop.
  The Plurality of Worlds of Lewis.
  The Princess Hoppy.
  Some Thing Black.
LEON S. ROUDIEZ, *French Fiction Revisited.*

VEDRANA RUDAN, *Night.*
STIG SÆTERBAKKEN, *Siamese.*
LYDIE SALVAYRE, *The Company of Ghosts.*
  Everyday Life.
  The Lecture.
  Portrait of the Writer as a Domesticated Animal.
  The Power of Flies.
LUIS RAFAEL SÁNCHEZ, *Macho Camacho's Beat.*
SEVERO SARDUY, *Cobra & Maitreya.*
NATHALIE SARRAUTE, *Do You Hear Them?*
  Martereau.
  The Planetarium.
ARNO SCHMIDT, *Collected Stories.*
  Nobodaddy's Children.
CHRISTINE SCHUTT, *Nightwork.*
GAIL SCOTT, *My Paris.*
DAMION SEARLS, *What We Were Doing and
  Where We Were Going.*
JUNE AKERS SEESE,
  Is This What Other Women Feel Too?
  What Waiting Really Means.
BERNARD SHARE, *Inish.*
  Transit.
AURELIE SHEEHAN, *Jack Kerouac Is Pregnant.*
VIKTOR SHKLOVSKY, *Knight's Move.*
  A Sentimental Journey: Memoirs 1917–1922.
  Energy of Delusion: A Book on Plot.
  Literature and Cinematography.
  Theory of Prose.
  Third Factory.
  Zoo, or Letters Not about Love.
JOSEF ŠKVORECKÝ, *The Engineer of Human Souls.*
CLAUDE SIMON, *The Invitation.*
GILBERT SORRENTINO, *Aberration of Starlight.*
  Blue Pastoral.
  Crystal Vision.
  Imaginative Qualities of Actual Things.
  Mulligan Stew.
  Pack of Lies.
  Red the Fiend.
  The Sky Changes.
  Something Said.
  Splendide-Hôtel.
  Steelwork.
  Under the Shadow.
W. M. SPACKMAN, *The Complete Fiction.*
ANDRZEJ STASIUK, *Fado.*
GERTRUDE STEIN, *Lucy Church Amiably.*
  The Making of Americans.
  A Novel of Thank You.
PIOTR SZEWC, *Annihilation.*
GONÇALO M. TAVARES, *Jerusalem.*
LUCIAN DAN TEODOROVICI, *Our Circus Presents . . . .*
STEFAN THEMERSON, *Hobson's Island.*
  The Mystery of the Sardine.
  Tom Harris.
JEAN-PHILIPPE TOUSSAINT, *The Bathroom.*
  Camera.
  Monsieur.
  Running Away.
  Television.
DUMITRU TSEPENEAG, *Pigeon Post.*
  The Necessary Marriage.
  Vain Art of the Fugue.
ESTHER TUSQUETS, *Stranded.*
DUBRAVKA UGRESIC, *Lend Me Your Character.*
  Thank You for Not Reading.
MATI UNT, *Brecht at Night*
  Diary of a Blood Donor.
  Things in the Night.
ÁLVARO URIBE AND OLIVIA SEARS, EDS.,
  The Best of Contemporary Mexican Fiction.
ELOY URROZ, *The Obstacles.*
LUISA VALENZUELA, *He Who Searches.*
PAUL VERHAEGHEN, *Omega Minor.*
MARJA-LIISA VARTIO, *The Parson's Widow.*
BORIS VIAN, *Heartsnatcher.*
ORNELA VORPSI, *The Country Where No One Ever Dies.*
AUSTRYN WAINHOUSE, *Hedyphagetica.*
PAUL WEST, *Words for a Deaf Daughter & Gala.*
CURTIS WHITE, *America's Magic Mountain.*
  The Idea of Home.
  Memories of My Father Watching TV.
  *Monstrous Possibility: An Invitation to
  Literary Politics.*
  Requiem.
DIANE WILLIAMS, *Excitability: Selected Stories.*
  Romancer Erector.
DOUGLAS WOOLF, *Wall to Wall.*
  Ya! & John-Juan.
JAY WRIGHT, *Polynomials and Pollen.*
  The Presentable Art of Reading Absence.
PHILIP WYLIE, *Generation of Vipers.*
MARGUERITE YOUNG, *Angel in the Forest.*
  Miss MacIntosh, My Darling.
REYOUNG, *Unbabbling.*
ZORAN ŽIVKOVIĆ, *Hidden Camera.*
LOUIS ZUKOFSKY, *Collected Fiction.*
SCOTT ZWIREN, *God Head.*

FOR A FULL LIST OF PUBLICATIONS, VISIT:
www.dalkeyarchive.com